FOR SURE AND CERTAIN

I DO NOT LOVE HENRY YODER

AN AMISH HOCKEY ROM-COM

JENNIFER SPREDEMANN

BRANDI GABRIEL

BLESSED PUBLISHING

For Sure and Certain I Do NOT Love Henry Yoder
(An Amish Hockey Rom-Com)

JENNIFER SPREDEMANN
BRANDI GABRIEL
© 2025

Get a FREE Amish story as my thank-you gift when you sign up for my newsletter at: www.jenniferspredemann.com

To our faithful readers. Thank you! We hope you love this foray into the Amish hockey world.

BOOKS BY JENNIFER SPREDEMANN

AMISH BY ACCIDENT TRILOGY

Amish by Accident

Englisch on Purpose (Prequel to *Amish by Accident*)

Christmas in Paradise (Sequel to *Amish by Accident*) (co-authored with Brandi Gabriel)

AMISH SECRETS SERIES

An Unforgivable Secret - Amish Secrets 1

A Secret Encounter - Amish Secrets 2

A Secret of the Heart - Amish Secrets 3

An Undeniable Secret - Amish Secrets 4

A Secret Sacrifice - Amish Secrets 5 (co-authored with Brandi Gabriel)

A Secret of the Soul - Amish Secrets 6

A Secret Christmas – Amish Secrets 2.5 (co-authored with Brandi Gabriel)

KING FAMILY SAGA (AMISH BIBLE ROMANCES)

An Amish Reward (Isaac)

An Amish Deception (Jacob)

An Amish Honor (Joseph)

AMISH COURTSHIP SERIES

A Forbidden Amish Courtship

A Widower's Amish Courtship

A Christmas Amish Courtship

An Englischer's Amish Courtship

A Seaside Amish Courtship

A Sister's Amish Courtship

AMISH HOCKEY ROM-COMS

For Sure and Certain I Do NOT Love Henry Yoder (2025)

I Might Just Be in Love with the Coach's Daughter (2025, Lord willing)

Can't Help Falling in Love with My Hockey Player Husband (2026, Lord Willing)

FAIRY TALES

The Princess and the Prayer Kapp (Cindy's Story & Rosabelle's Story)

OTHER

Learning to Love – Saul's Story (Sequel to Chloe's Revelation)

Her Amish Identity

An Unexpected Christmas Gift

The Crimson Dress

BOOKS BY J.E.B. SPREDEMANN

AMISH GIRLS SERIES

Joanna's Struggle

Danika's Journey

Chloe's Revelation

Susanna's Surprise

Annie's Decision

Abigail's Triumph

Brooke's Quest

Leah's Legacy

A Christmas of Mercy – Amish Girls Holiday

BOOKS BY BRANDI GABRIEL
THE ORPHAN BRIDE

The Cowhand's Bride (A Marriage of Convenience story)

If He Only Knew (with Michelynn Christy aka Jennifer Spredemann)

Amish Girls Series (co-authored with Jennifer Spredemann and Emily Spredemann)

Unofficial Glossary of Pennsylvania Dutch Words/Phrases

Ach – Oh

Ach du liebe – Expression similar to "Oh, my goodness!" or "Oh, dear!"

Ain't not/Ain't so – Right? Or Isn't that so?

Bann – Shunning/excommunication

Boppli/Bopplin – Baby/Babies

Bruder/Brieder – Brother/Brothers

Buss – Kiss

Daed/Dat – Dad

Denki – Thanks

Der Herr – The Lord

Der Welt – The world

Dietsch – Pennsylvania German

Dochder(n) – Daughter(s)

Dumm – Dumb

Dummkopp – Dummy

Eck – Corner table at an Amish wedding reception, where the bride and groom sit

Englischer – A non-Amish person

Ferhoodled – Crazy, scatterbrained, mind is elsewhere *(Don't you love this fun word?)*

For-gut (as in clothing) – Nice/church clothes

Fraa – Wife/Missus

Geh – Go

G'may – Members of an Amish fellowship

Gott – God

Grossdawdi (Dawdi) – Grandpa

Grossmammi (Mammi) – Grandma

Gut – Good

Haus – House

Hochmut – Proud

Jah – Yes/Yeah

Kapp – Amish head covering for women

Kind/Kinner – Child/Children

Kumm – Come

Lieb – Love (as in sweetheart/sweety)

Maed/Maedel – Girls/Girl

Mamm – Mom

Mei – My

Nee – No

Ordnung – Rules followed by the Amish church (varies according to district)

Schatzi – Sweetheart

Schweschder(n) – Sister(s)

Sohn – Son

The familye way – Pregnant

Vatter – Father

Vell – Well

Verboten – Forbidden

Wunderbaar – Wonderful

Youngie – Young folks/youth group

AUTHORS' NOTE

About the Amish:

The Amish/Mennonite people and their communities differ one from another. There are, in fact, no two Amish communities exactly alike. It is this premise on which this book is written. We have taken cautious steps to ensure the authenticity of Amish practices and customs. Old Order Amish and New Order Amish may be portrayed in this work of fiction and may differ from some communities. Although the book may be set in a certain locality, the practices featured in the book may not necessarily reflect that particular district's beliefs or culture. This book is purely fictional and built around a fictional community, even though you may see similarities to real-life people, practices, and occurrences.

We, as *Englischers*, can learn a lot from the Plain People and their simple way of life. Their hard work, close-knit family life, and concern for others are to be applauded. As the Lord wills, may this special culture continue to be respected and remain so for many centuries to come, and may the light of God's salvation reach their hearts.

About Hockey:

The Indianapolis Icebergs (Indy Ice) are a fictional professional hockey team. Since Indiana doesn't have a professional hockey team according to our research/knowledge, we thought it would be fun to give them one. ☺

Although we have conducted extensive research, we by no means claim to be hockey experts, so please forgive any mistakes! (And if you find any, please notify us via *private* message. Thanks!)

CHAPTER 1

ELLIE

There's no one I can't stand more than Henry Yoder.

I know. It's not very Amish of me to say that because everyone and their *grossmammi* knows that Amish have to forgive everything. It's not even an option. It's built into our DNA. But, with Henry, I just can't make myself.

I don't even want to look his way. And I won't.

Because if I do, I'll get trapped in his *dumm* mesmerizing sea-green eyes.

Then he'll lift his *dumm* cocky brow and wink at me.

And then his *dumm* kissable lips will twitch at the corners.

No.

Not kissable.

Disgusting.

Jah.

Because Henry Yoder does *not* have kissable lips. Nor does he deserve a second glance.

Not since he stole my lunchbox in fourth grade. And smirked as he ate my peanut butter and jelly sandwich right in front of me. Then he proceeded to consume my entire bag of barbeque chips. *Barbeque, y'all!* Then my fuji apple. Then, last but not least, he devoured my beloved whoopie pie.

Jah, the whoopie pie was an unforgivable offense for sure and certain. And he had the audacity to lick his fingers right in front of me!

And has he ever apologized? No. No, he has not. Not even once.

Like he's proud about what he did. And everyone knows pride is a sin. One of the worst, actually. After all, it is the sin that made the devil fall. Not to mention, it goes against the *Ordnung* too. *Jah*, Henry Yoder is definitely full of pride.

Just one more reason not to like him.

No apology. No forgiveness.

Upset couldn't begin to describe how I felt that day. I was humiliated in front of my friends, but I never told the teacher about Henry's antics. The truth is our substitute teacher that day was kind of mean. And as angry as I was at Henry, I didn't want him to get a switching. But I am determined to pay him back. Someday.

"Ellie, Henry Yoder asked if you'd ride home with him tonight. Again." My brother Elijah pulls me into the hallway of the Grabers' home, a scowl on his face. "One of these days, you should just go with him."

"Not on his life." I move to the side, but Elijah blocks my way. "Now, if you'll excuse me, Mary and Lizzie need me on the team."

He stops me with a hand on my shoulder. "What should I tell him?"

"Same as the last seven times he asked. No."

"*Kumm* on, Ellie. Won't you give him just one chance? One. That's it. He's going to keep asking until you say yes."

That is just *dumm*. Like he will still be asking when I'm thirty-two and happily married.

"Nope." I move past my brother and hurry to the back door toward the volleyball game that has surely begun without me by now.

Would Henry *ever* leave me alone? One would think he would've gotten the hint by now. But no. He keeps asking. Like he's trying to wear me down. Well,

I've got news for him. He's not going to win at this game.

Of course, Henry Yoder would have to be at the net opposite me. And, of course, that attractive dark lock of hair would have to fall over his forehead. And, of course, that cocky grin displayed a row of perfectly straight white teeth.

No, the dark lock of hair is *not* attractive. Henry Yoder is *not* attractive. Even if half the single women in the *g'may* swoon over him every time his buggy rolls up to one of the young folks' gatherings.

Besides, I'm beginning to acquire a certain fondness for crooked teeth. Crooked teeth have more character. And white teeth? So overrated. That only means the guy doesn't drink coffee. Who could live with someone who couldn't appreciate a decent cup of coffee? And who is looking for perfectly straight white teeth anyway? Not me. No, siree.

CHAPTER 2

HENRY

I admit that I've had a crush on Ellie Petersheim for as long as I can remember.

I also admit that I probably should have chosen someone easier to get. Because Ellie Petersheim is tough as nails.

But, working in construction, nails just happen to be my specialty. And I love a good challenge.

I'm not even sure why she doesn't like me. All the other girls seem to like me just fine.

But maybe that's *why* I like Ellie so much. She's *not* just like the other girls. She has a mind of her own.

Just that spark in her hazel eyes is enough to light my fire. Challenge accepted.

How hard could it be, right?

Growing up, *Mamm* said I could charm just about anybody into anything. And that's exactly what I plan to do to get Ellie Petersheim to marry me.

But she can't suspect what I'm up to. Because if she suspects anything, that will be the end of that.

Nope, I need to take her by surprise.

Maybe I should have a chat with her brother Elijah to find out why she detests me so much.

Whatever I do, it's going to have to be fast. Because I overheard Simon Byler say he plans to ask her on a buggy ride.

It seems like no matter how many times I ask, she turns me down flat every time. I plan on wearing her down, so she'll eventually ride with me. She can't say no forever, right? But that strategy doesn't seem to be working so far. I might have to come up with a different plan.

So, a chat with Eli it is. He's never mentioned anything before about why Ellie can't stand my presence. Would he even know why his *schweschder* doesn't like me?

I sigh and make my way over to Elijah after the singing. "What did she say?" I ask, but I already know the answer. Still, a guy can hope.

"Sorry, Henry." The pity in his eyes doesn't escape my notice.

"Has she said *anything* to you about why she detests me so much?" I keep an eye out behind Elijah's back as Simon Byler makes his way toward Ellie. I growl, causing Elijah to look in his sister's direction.

"*Nee.*" Elijah studies me, a little too intently, like when we're out on the pond playing ice hockey and he's about to go for a goal. For no good reason, the accusation in his mien makes me squirm.

"What?" I don't like being accused of something I know nothing about, which is exactly how Elijah is looking at me.

"Did you do something to her?"

Thinking about Eli's question, I scratch my thin layer of facial hair, which seems to have grown since this morning when I shaved and donned my *for-gut* clothes for visiting and tonight's gathering. Since our church is only conducted every other week, our next service won't be until the following Sunday. "Not that I know of."

"Then why don't you talk to her?"

Jah, like that has ever worked with Ellie. "She won't give me the time of day. Just huffs and storms away."

"That ain't normal behavior for *mei schweschder*. You must've done *something*." Elijah's eyes squint at me like he is trying to determine if I am the devil or not.

I'm not. And as far as I know, I'm a halfway decent guy. "How can I get her to talk to me if she scurries away every time I'm near?"

Elijah shrugs. "Beats me. What if you did something to make her jealous?"

"Like what?"

"Take one of her friends home."

I have taken a couple of *maed* home on occasion. It never worked in the past. Nevertheless, I think about his suggestion. "How will that make her jealous when she has no desire to let me court her?"

"*Jah*, I guess you've got a point." Elijah frowns. "I have an idea"—he leans over and lowers his voice—"but you can't tell her that it came from me because then she'll hate both of us."

Hate is such a strong, ugly word. Although Ellie detests me something wonderful, I doubt she would actually *hate* someone. That's not the Amish way. But still... "I don't want her to hate me."

"She already hates *you, dummkopp*, so you don't have anything to lose. I just don't want *mei schweschder* to hate me too. I have to live with her, you know."

"*Wunderbaar.*" I roll my eyes. "I'd love to hear

whatever grand advice you have that might make her hate me more."

He whispers something in my ear.

"Do you think that would work?" My lips curl up at his suggestion. Not necessarily a bad one.

"It would at least get her to talk to you, *ain't not*?"

"Do you think Simon will go for it?"

"I think so. He's been saving his pennies for a new dashboard and radio for his buggy. If you offer him a decent amount, I'm sure he'll jump at the chance to make some quick cash."

I'm not convinced Elijah's plan will work, but I suppose it's worth a shot if I can get Ellie to talk to me for once.

"Okay." I take a deep breath and eye Simon. For Ellie, I can do this.

I begin striding over to Simon, thankful that Ellie's back is toward me. *Jah*, her back is always toward me, so I'm not surprised. But Ellie has a nice back, so I don't really mind. But staring into her eyes is the stuff my dreams are made of.

No, I'm serious.

Just last night, I had a dream. *Nee*, it wasn't the kind of dream that I read about one time in a famous poem about not judging others by their appearance.

Nor was it like Joseph's dream in the Bible. My dream was different.

It was about me and Ellie. The two of us were down by the pond after my unicorn dropped us off.

Jah, I know. There's no such thing as unicorns, but anything is possible in a dream.

Anyhow, it was just Ellie and me by the pond. And there was a waterfall too, that kind of shot out of a tree. With peacocks in it. The peacocks were in the tree, not in the waterfall. Don't ask. I don't know where the unicorn went, but somehow, it grew wings and flew off into the sky and disappeared behind some clouds.

And Ellie and me, well, we just stood by the pond gazing into each other's eyes. I didn't touch her. I didn't kiss her. I just stared at her. And she stared at me.

And then I woke up. The smile stayed fixed on my face the entire day. My cheeks actually ached. Well, until I saw Ellie and she turned her nose up at me. Again.

So, yes, I am stooping low enough to pay Simon to let me use his buggy and take Ellie home. It is underhanded and it will quite possibly make Ellie like me even less, if that is possible. I don't like the underhanded part.

But I have to try, don't I? I can't just let this opportunity slip through my fingers. What if she rides home with Simon tonight, falls desperately in love with him, and signs up for baptism classes this fall? Then where will I be? I can't let that happen.

So, here I am, approaching the man who managed to get Ellie to say yes to a buggy ride. What does this guy have that I don't? "Simon. May I have a word with you?"

He shrugs. "Sure. What's up?"

I tilt my head toward the door so we can speak in private. He follows me with his plate of snacks, smacking with every bite he takes. *Really, Ellie? You're choosing this guy over me?*

I get right to the point. "May I use your buggy tonight?"

He scratches his head. "Uh...I don't know. I was going to take Ellie home tonight."

"I can take her home." Okay, so maybe I sound a little too eager.

"What's wrong with your rig?"

"Nothing at all."

He scratches his head. "I'm confused."

I attempt an explanation. "I was going to ask you to drive my buggy home, then I'll pick it up after I drop off Ellie."

Simon sticks out his hand and touches my forehead. "Are you feeling okay?"

"*Jah*, I'm fine." I bat his hand away. "I just want a chance with Ellie, that's all."

"So, why didn't *you* ask to take her home?"

"I did, but she turned me down flat."

Simon laughs. And laughs. And laughs.

I want to slug the guy, no matter how deep my Amish roots run. But I keep my cool, because Amish men don't just go around getting aggressive. We're cool, passive, non-resistant. That's the refrain I'm repeating to myself as my hands clench.

Simon finally reins in his amusement. "So, let me get this straight. Ellie won't ride with *you*—Henry Yoder—so you want to pretend to be *me* so she'll ride with you?" Simon shakes his head. "I never thought I'd see the day a *maedel* would say no to Henry Yoder. Why Ellie when you can have your pick?"

"She's the only one I want. And I'm willing to pay you for your inconvenience."

His eyebrow lifts and I know I have his attention now. "Bribery?"

I shrug. "Something like that. Come on, I just want a chance with her."

"You must really like her if you're this desperate."

"I do." But maybe I shouldn't have admitted that.

Desperation doesn't usually make for good bargaining power.

"Okay." Simon tosses his plate into the trash and shoves his hands into his pockets. "A hundred dollars."

"A hundred dollars? Are you crazy?" I squint at him. "I'll give you fifty."

"Make it one fifty."

"A hundred dollars it is." I growl.

"*Gut.*" Simon holds out his hand, palm open.

"I don't have it all right now. I only have forty bucks on me." I pull out my wallet and slide Simon forty dollars. I hate being without any money.

"You're not going to pull a fast one on me, are you?" Simon examines me.

"I said I would pay you, and I will. Besides, you know where I live, and I see you every week. Now, please drive your rig up to wherever you agreed to meet Ellie, then we'll switch out places. Be sure to park in the shadow."

"Okay, I'll let her know I'm heading out. I'm driving to the side where the door to the mud room is." Simon frowns. "She's going to be mad at me for doing this."

"*Nee.* She'll be mad at *me.*" I rub my facial hair. Maybe this isn't such a hot idea. But since I already have my pucks in order, I may as well go for the goal.

Besides, I doubt Simon would be willing to give me my money back and let me off the hook.

I make my way outside, then hop into Simon's buggy while he goes to fetch my rig. I wait until Ellie descends the steps, making sure to stay in the shadow and keep my hat low. The buggy dips on the opposite side as the girl of my dreams plants herself on the seat beside me.

My heart feels like it might just gallop right out of my chest. Ellie Petersheim is sitting beside me.

I signal to the horse and jiggle the reins with my clammy hands, and that's when I know she knows.

"Henry Yoder? What are you...why are *you* in Simon's buggy? I agreed to ride home with *him*, not *you*." Venom laces her words. "I told Elijah to tell you no. I don't appreciate whatever kind of trick you are trying to play."

My hope plummets. Although I somewhat expected her words, hearing them spoken to my face stings. But I'm not about to give up. "Aw, come on, Ellie. You wouldn't ride with me otherwise. What else could I have done?"

"Respect my wishes." She demands, "Let me out. Now."

I don't think I've ever seen her more mad.

But I'm not giving up. Not now that I finally have

her next to me. "No. Not until we've had a civil conversation," I challenge. "How else could I have gotten you to talk to me?"

She huffs, crosses her arms over her chest, then turns away. Great. The silent treatment. Just what I was hoping for. *Way to go, Yoder.*

We ride in silence for a little while, because I don't dare speak. I'll wait until she's ready. We're far enough away from the young folks' gathering that darkness surrounds us. But I keep quiet and wait until she is ready to speak.

"Why are you doing this?"

I was not expecting a sob to escape her lips. It's my undoing. The last thing I desire is for Ellie to be in tears. I acquiesce and pull over onto the road's shoulder. I gentle my voice. "Hey. Hey, now."

Surprisingly, she lets me gather her into my arms. Perhaps my calm tone has softened her toward me just a little bit.

"It's okay," I soothe, stroking her back. "I'm sorry, Ellie. I never meant to upset you." Now, I'm wondering...does she truly hate me like Elijah said earlier?

She looks up at me as tears streak her face.

I thumb them away, her face cradled in my hands. We lock eyes and when her breath hitches ever so softly, I can hardly refrain from dipping my head and tasting her full pink lips. *Jah*, self-control has never been my strong suit. Nor has common sense, apparently.

She responds in kind at first, and I'm in heaven. Maybe she doesn't hate me like I thought. Then she seems to come to her senses when she remembers it's me, and pushes me away.

"Henry Yoder, don't you ever do that again!" She skitters out of the buggy like her dress is on fire and shoots off down the road in the opposite direction.

I turn Simon's horse and rig around and follow after her. When we are side by side, I coax, "Ellie, come on. You shouldn't be out here walking in the dark alone. It's not safe. Please get in."

She completely ignores me and continues her determined pace. She finally speaks. "I'm not talking to you, Henry Yoder!"

"That sounds like talking to me. But if you prefer, we can do more kissing." *Jah*, I am pushing it, and I know it.

"Ugh, you have to be the most annoying person that ever lived!" She turns an about face and begins walking the opposite direction.

I flip a U with Simon's buggy and head in the same direction. Now that I am side by side with her again, I can resume our mostly one-sided conversation. *Use your charm, Henry. Get her to smile.*

"I think you might be *slightly* exaggerating. Take Ernest Kinsinger, for instance. Remember he used to blow his nose really loud right next to people and then leave his snot rags on other peoples' desks then blame someone else for it? Now *that* was annoying. Then, how about Martin—"

"I get the point." She grinds out the words. "And you're proving mine."

She veers off into the cornfield.

Oh, no, you don't!

There is no way on earth I am going to let her tromp through a cornfield. Alone. In the middle of the night. I sigh, then bring the buggy to a halt and jump down. "You leave me no choice."

Ellie must hear me coming because she quickens her pace to almost a full-on run.

"Ellie, come on!" I charge after her. "You can't just run through a cornfield in the middle of the night. There are wild animals out here."

Without thinking, I swoop in, twist her body around, and hoist her over my shoulder. I pivot, hauling her back to the buggy.

"Henry Yoder, *you're* the wild animal. Let me

down right now!" She pounds my back like her life is in mortal danger.

I groan, sure and certain she is leaving bruises. But I don't care. I have Ellie Petersheim in my arms, and I'm not about to let her go. "Settle down, my little banshee."

"How dare you! Put me down." She wriggles to no avail.

"Not until we talk. And I'm taking you home whether you want me to or not. What kind of a man would I be leaving you out here alone in the dark? I'm probably saving your life. It's ridiculous trying to run off when we're nowhere near civilization."

"Oh, so now you think I'm ridiculous and you're a hero?"

The ire in her voice doesn't escape my notice. "Why do you hate me so much?"

"I don't *hate* you, Henry Yoder. It's not Amish. It goes against the *Ordnung*."

I sneer. "Right. Then why do you dislike me and ignore me at every turn?"

She erupts in a mirthless laugh and squirms. "You have to ask?"

I tighten my hold, ignoring the thrill of having her so close to me, her feminine scent tantalizing my senses. Well, it might be thrilling if she didn't insist on pounding on my back. "Hey, I asked you to stop in the cornfield. Nicely, I might add. I even said please. Can I help it if you wouldn't listen?"

"You can't just haul women over your shoulder like a sack of potatoes!"

I shrug, then chuckle. "Seems to me, I can."

I silently thank God for my size and strength. Because I'm pretty sure Simon wouldn't be able to carry Ellie like this.

"Ugh!" This time her teeth sink into the backside of my upper arm.

"Ow! You don't play fair, woman."

"And *you* do?"

"Almost there, my feisty little potato. Or maybe I'm the potato since you're obviously attempting to eat me." I chuckle.

"Quit with the annoying nicknames, will you?"

"I thought it was cute."

"You would, you brute."

"Aww, now who's using cute nicknames?"

She snorts. "Only *you* would interpret the word *brute* as a term of endearment."

"I'm not sure I know what that means." I actually do, but bantering with Ellie is fun. I never know what she'll come up with next.

"Figures." I can't see her expression, but I can

picture her rolling her eyes. Not literally, of course. Because that would just be weird. "Ever thought of opening a book once in a while instead of spending every spare moment playing hockey on the pond?"

"The thought never occurred to me. Besides, the pond is only frozen for so long. I have to take advantage of it while I can."

We approach Simon's rig.

"Okay. Am I going to set you down in the buggy nicely or am I going to have to hold you in my lap? What's it going to be?" I lean back and lift an eyebrow. "Choice is yours. Of course, the latter sounds funner if you ask me."

"Just. Put. Me. Down." Ellie grounds out the words.

I'll admit that I love a good challenge. "Fine. But don't go anywhere. If you'll allow me to, I'll take you safely home."

"Fine."

I side-eye her. "Really? You won't try to run? Or bonk me on the head with a rock?"

"Not unless you try to kiss me again."

"If I recall correctly, you were kissing me back." I smirk.

"Only because it was a natural reflex. I *never* would have kissed you otherwise."

"I'm not sure I believe that, Ellie Petersheim. I think that deep down, you like me. Maybe even think I'm hot."

Ellie laughs. "You're so full of yourself, Henry Yoder. Just another reason I don't like you. Or think you're hot. Hot guys aren't full of themselves. You're just *hochmut*."

I snort. "You want me to be all boring like Simon Byler?"

"Exactly."

I eye her curiously. "And you think Simon is *hot*?"

"I didn't say *that*. Just that he's not prideful."

I hop up into the buggy, then gently set her down beside me. For the first time in my life, I wish buggies had seat belts. Because, if Ellie was to bolt again, I'd at least have the unbuckling of a safety belt to warn me.

I maneuver Simon's buggy back onto the road. Thankfully, Ellie is true to her word and doesn't bolt. "Hmm. I guess you really don't know him, then, do you?"

"I know him just fine."

"Name one thing Simon has that I don't." I challenge, because I really want to know what she sees in the guy. It isn't that he's a bad person, he just isn't right for Ellie.

"He's nice."

"And I'm not?"

"Hardly."

I scratch my head, trying to recall a time in my life that I haven't been nice. Because I feel like I truly was —or am—a nice person. I'm thoroughly baffled.

"What do you mean? Name one time I wasn't nice." I stare at her. Man, she has pretty eyes. It is hard to look away.

But I should have because now her eyes dance with fire as though she wants to torch me. I half expect lasers to come shooting out, like I saw in a movie one time.

"I'll give you one hint, Henry. Whoopie pie."

I love it when she says my name. Although, admittedly, it would be better if it rolled off her tongue with affection and wasn't laced with bitterness. But, hey, I'll take what I can get.

"I have no idea what you're referring to. I love whoopie pies."

"Ugh. Never mind. You are *so* clueless." She turns in her seat, jamming her arms across her chest, shunning my presence. Again.

This evening isn't exactly going the way I'd hoped.

"Or...do *you* not like whoopie pies?"

"I happen to love whoopie pies, Henry Yoder." She

glares at me like I'm supposed to get some hidden meaning behind her words.

I sit there "clueless" like Ellie oh so gently pointed out, wishing the horse would slow down so our ride would take longer. But no matter how I try to rein the gelding in, he seems to have only one speed.

Before I know it, we're pulling into the Petersheims' driveway. And my time with Ellie is up. I have to think of something to say and quick. Otherwise, who knows if I'll ever get this opportunity again? Because I'm sure and certain she isn't about to invite me inside.

"What kind?" I blurt out.

"What are you talking about?"

"What kind of whoopie pies are your favorite?"

"I like all kinds. Lemon, strawberry, chocolate with peanut butter filling." She shrugs.

"I don't know if I've ever had any of those kinds. But I could imagine they would be delicious." If only I can talk her into making me some. But I better not push my luck.

"You would. Probably steal them right off the grocery shelf if you saw them at the store."

Her comment is like a slap to the face. "I'd never steal whoopie pies. Or anything, for that matter." I scratch my chin in confusion.

At that, she jumps out of the buggy and bolts toward the door of her house.

"Ellie, wait!" I call out in desperation. "Aren't you going to invite me inside?"

But it's too late. She'd already stepped inside, and the screen door shuts with a thud. I'm not about to follow where I'm not wanted.

"I'll take that as a no," I mumble.

I sigh, turn the rig around, and head out of her driveway and onto the road. Our conversation plays over and over in my mind. I attempt to put the pieces of the puzzle together, but fail at making sense of Ellie's behavior and words.

Then an idea strikes like a puck to the forehead.

Yes, that's it!

CHAPTER 3

*H*ENRY

Before I even see her, my *schweschder's* annoying cackle hits my ears.

Ivy *would* have to enter the kitchen just after I'd donned my *mamm's* frilly pink apron.

"What in the world are you doing, *bruder*?" She says through a snort.

I hold up the cookbook. "Learning how to make whoopie pies."

She pops up onto the counter, backside first, and squints her eyes. "Who are you and what have you done with my little brother?"

"Ellie Petersheim loves whoopie pies," I say, as though that should explain everything.

"And?"

"And I want to make her the best whoopie pies she's ever tasted."

That comment elicits another round of giggles from my oh-so-supportive sister.

"Is that so unbelievable?" I study the recipe in front of me. Surely, whoopie pies can't be *that* hard to make. Right?

"Being that I've never seen you in the kitchen with an apron and mixing bowl before, I'd say it would take nothing short of a miracle. You think you can just become the world's best baker overnight?"

"A miracle? Really? They don't seem *that* difficult." My lips twist as I read the ingredients. Flour, baking soda, unsweetened cocoa, salt, butter... "Do we have vegetable shortening?"

"*Jah*, we should."

I open up the pantry and frown. Three hundred and twenty-two items stare back at me. "Umm...where is it?"

Ivy rolls her eyes. "You're so blind."

She reaches into the cupboard and pulls out the large white tub in front of my face, then hefts it onto the counter with a thunk.

"*Denki, schwes.*"

Ivy grimaces. "I wouldn't use vegetable shortening for those."

I stare at my *schweschder*. "But the recipe calls for it." I shove the book under her nose to make my point.

"Fine. Don't listen to me." She pushes the recipe book away and shrugs. "You said you wanted to make *the best* whoopie pies she's ever tasted, but I guess you know better than your older sister, who has been making them since she was five. You're the expert, bro." She pats my shoulder then walks out of the kitchen.

I'm confused as I stare at her walking off. I desperately want to make the best whoopie pies ever. I *need* to make the best whoopie pies ever.

If I don't make the best whoopie pies ever then Ellie won't fall in love with me and she might marry someone like Simon Byler then I'll have to see them at church every other Sunday with their entire clan of little ones and I would still be a bachelor because I don't want to marry anyone other than Ellie Petersheim and I would just stare longingly in Ellie's direction hating myself for the rest of my life because I didn't make the best whoopie pies ever.

That. Cannot. Happen.

Desperation overtakes me, and I throw the cookbook onto the counter and run after Ivy. "Wait! Can you help me?" I jump in front of her to stop her trek toward her bedroom.

"It's going to cost you."

Great. I don't know how I always get stuck in the middle of Ivy's schemes, but here I am again. "What this time?"

"I need you to cover for me." Her saucy grin tells me she's up to no good.

"*Ivy.*" I use my *I should be the big brother* warning tone.

"Don't judge me."

"You're not going out with Jude, are you?" I narrow my gaze at her. Our *Englisch* neighbor has turned more than one Amish young woman's head, but he signed on with the hockey league a year or so ago and has been away for a while.

Her look turns wistful. "Jude is back home again?"

"I'm not sure. I thought he was coming home for a visit this week." I point at her. "And you're changing the subject."

"Maybe. Is he playing hockey with the guys this week?"

"I don't know. Maybe?"

Hopefully, my Ellie hasn't taken a shine to the

popular *Englischer* too. Although Jude and I have become great friends over the years, this is a hill I am willing to die on. Nobody is going to steal Ellie Petersheim's heart. I have every intention of making her my *fraa*.

And it would start with making her the best whoopie pies she's ever tasted. Which brings me back to the issue at hand.

"What do you need me to do for you, Ivy?" Time is running out. I sigh and tap my foot, knowing I won't like her answer.

"Distract *Mamm*."

"*Mamm* isn't here. Is she?"

Have I missed something? Is she taking a nap? Naps aren't something Mom usually indulges in but she'd taken a few since *Dat* passed on to glory. Losing someone special did that to a body—zapped all your strength so that you had no choice but to stop and rest and cry. Don't ask me how I know.

"She's coming home tomorrow, remember?"

Right. I didn't realize what day it was. How quickly I forget about everything else when Ellie Petersheim is on the brain.

"I'm glad I got that wood split and stacked." I rub the back of my neck, wondering if I've forgotten anything else I was supposed to do while *Mamm* has been gone. Things were so much better when *Dat* was alive. When I didn't feel like I had the world on my shoulders. But I won't dwell on that right now. I can't.

Not when I need to make the best whoopie pies ever.

Ivy continues, "Anyway, I've been making your meals since she's been gone and I'm in need of a break."

"What do you mean? A break?" I stare at Ivy. What is my *schweschder* up to?

"Let's just say I got an offer I can't refuse. I'll be back home on Wednesday."

"Where are you going, Ivy? And who with?" Yes, my big-brother complex is kicking in again.

Ever since *Dat* went on to glory, I feel like I have to fill his boots somehow. And that includes watching out for my *schweschder*, even though she is the older sibling.

"If I tell you, then you might feel like you have to lie for me. It's better if you don't know."

"You have me worried, Ivy. I don't like this." I put my hands on her shoulders and look her in the eye. I may be the younger of us two, but I have the advantage of my father's height and broad shoulders. "What's

Mamm going to say when she comes home and you're not here?"

"*Mamm* will be preoccupied with *Mammi* and *Dawdi's* situation. She probably won't even notice I'm gone." She has a point. Last time *Mamm* returned home from a visit, it seemed like her mind was still in Ohio. But still.

"Of course, she'll notice. And what am I supposed to say when she asks?"

"That I'm fine and I'll be home in a couple of days."

"But how will I know you're fine, Ivy? She's going to want to know where you are."

Ivy smirks and pats me on the shoulder. "Which is exactly why I'm not telling you. I'll call you. Will that set your mind at ease?"

"Twice a day." Yes, I am overprotective. But I can't help it.

My sister and mother and maternal grandparents are pretty much all I have left in this world. And at the rate things are going, I'm not sure how long our grandparents will be with us. I hardly see them as it is.

Hmm, maybe after Ellie and I get hitched, we can make a trip out to Ohio to visit them. Which reminds me. Whoopie pies.

Ivy rolls her eyes. "Fine. I'll try to call you as often as I can. No promises, though."

"Now. Will you *please* help me make Ellie Petersheim the best whoopie pies ever?"

"I hope she knows what a special girl she is. Any man who would make his woman whoopie pies is a keeper. She'll love you forever." Ivy grins.

If only…

CHAPTER 4

ELLIE

No matter what I do, I can't get that stupid amazing kiss from Henry Yoder out of my head.

The look of compassion in his eyes and the gentleness of his touch are what did me in. It was like he...*cared*.

I'm worried about my sanity now. Because I *knew* where we were heading, and I didn't stop it. *Why* didn't I stop it? Am I getting sucked into Henry's charms?

It would be much easier if Henry's kiss had been terrible. Why couldn't the kiss have been terrible? Like that time Arlen Yutzy kissed me on the playground with his new braces. But no. Henry's kiss just *had* to be amazing.

Now, I'll have to face Henry again when he and Elijah and the other guys play hockey at Henry's pond later. I'll just have to skate on the girls' end the whole time and pretend Henry Yoder doesn't exist.

Right.

"Ellie, do you know what this is all about?" *Mamm* calls up the stairs.

I push my reminiscing aside, wipe the last of the sleep crusties from my eyes, and move to the top of the stairs. I peer down at *Mamm*, a foil covered plate in her hand.

I have no idea why *Mamm* is asking *me*. "Am I supposed to?"

"It's got your name on it." *Mamm* holds up a piece of lined paper.

I stare at the plate, puzzled. "Where did it come from?"

"It was on the front steps this morning. It's a wonder the cats didn't find it."

"What's in it?"

"I don't know. It doesn't have *my* name on it. Why don't you come check?"

I glance down at my nightgown. "Are the boys inside?"

"They've already headed out to do chores. *Someone* overslept." *Mamm's* accusatory tone makes me squirm.

Jah, I didn't want to wake up from my dream. The one where Henry's lips—

Ach! What on earth am I doing? This is Henry Yoder, for crying out loud! The one I haven't been able to stand since fourth grade. Now, I'm dreaming about kissing him? I think I really do need to have my head examined.

Sure, Henry Yoder is devastatingly good looking—probably the handsomest man I know—but still. That is no excuse to waste away the morning fantasizing about how *wunderbaar* his lips would feel against mine again. Or how much strength his arms exhibited when he hauled me over his broad shoulder. Or how nice his—

I clear my throat to demand my thoughts get back on track. *Ach*, I'm a complete and utter mess! Just one more reason to steer clear of Henry today.

I shake my head as I notice *Mamm* eyeing me, a quizzical look on her face. No doubt she's trying to figure out why I'm so *ferhoodled* this morning. Then I remember my nightgown. "Let me change right quick, in case the boys return."

"*Nee*, just *kumm* down and see what it is. The suspense is killing me."

I laugh at *Mamm's* eagerness. "Okay."

I hurry down the stairs and retrieve the plate from *Mamm's* hand. I study my name on the note, then realize there is more written on the other side.

Roses are red, violets are blue. These whoopie pies were made specially for you.

"*Ach*, that's so sweet!" *Mamm* peers over my shoulder, her hand on her heart.

"*Mamm*, you're not supposed to spy." I huff. It is nearly impossible to get even a second of privacy in this family.

"Do you know who they're from?" *Mamm* did *not* just bounce on her toes.

Oh, no. I can see it in *Mamm's* eyes, clear as day. She is already picking out material for my wedding dress.

I. Am. Doomed.

But there is no way on earth I'd *ever* marry Henry Yoder—no matter how delicious his kisses are.

"It doesn't matter." I open the trash can and dump the entire plate inside.

"Ellie Petersheim! You should be ashamed of yourself." *Mamm* hurries to salvage the whoopie pies. Not that they're ruined, since there is a layer of plastic wrap under the foil.

"I don't want them. He's just trying to butter me up." I squint at the whoopie pies as though they are to blame for Henry's insolence.

Mamm claps her hands. "So, they *are* from a *bu*! I knew it!"

"They're just from Henry Yoder." I smack my hand over my mouth. Great. Now, I will *never* hear the end of it. Never. *Mamm* might just love Henry even more than Elijah, and he's my brother.

"What a sweet, sweet boy! You know I've always been fond of Henry."

"He's not a boy anymore, *Mamm*." Not by the way he lifted me over his broad shoulders. Or carried me in his muscular arms. His masculine scented body wash—or whatever it was—still teases my senses. Nope, definitely *not* a boy.

I sigh.

"I knew you two would end up together. I just knew it. I can't wait to talk to Martha Yoder about this." *Mamm* reaches for her bonnet.

"*Mamm, nee!* You can't talk to Henry's *mamm*. And Henry and I are *not* going to end up together!" I probably sound like a toddler throwing a temper tantrum, but this is ridiculous. No matter how many years *Mamm* and Martha Yoder plot against me, I am *not* going to marry Henry Yoder.

He may be irresistible to *Mamm* and all the other young women in the *g'may*, but I'm not about to fall for his charms. And it will take a whole lot more than a sorry plate of *dumm* whoopie pies to win me over.

Sounds of boot steps in the mudroom send me scurrying back to my bedroom upstairs to get dressed. The way this morning is going, Elijah will be walking through the door with Henry at his side. And the last thing I need is for Henry to see me with my hair down and in my nightgown.

I release a sigh of relief when I only hear my *brieder*. Hopefully, I won't have to see Henry until ice skating this evening, and even then I plan to avoid him at all costs.

"Wow! *Mamm*, these are the best whoopie pies you've ever made." I catch my brother's voice through the vent between my room and the kitchen below. "Maybe even the best I've ever had."

"I didn't make them," *Mamm* admits. "They were a gift for your *schweschder*."

I picture *Mamm's* eyebrows lifting and a dreamy smile on her face.

Please don't let her tell him the whoopie pies are

from Henry. I utter the silent prayer. Mercifully, *Mamm* doesn't expound.

"Ellie, I'm eating all your whoopie pies." Elijah calls up the stairs. "Tell whichever of your friends who made these that I want to marry her."

I giggle. If he only knew.

When the kitchen is quiet again, I sneak back downstairs. I glance outside to see *Mamm* carrying a load of laundry to the clothesline. *Wunderbaar,* she must've abandoned her mission to visit Henry's *mamm.* I look both ways to see if I am truly alone, then reach for one of Henry's whoopie pies.

There are several different kinds to choose from, it seems. All the kinds I mentioned to Henry on our buggy ride last night. I sigh. It *is* a thoughtful gesture. Even I can admit that. I grab the lemon one first and bite into it.

I close my eyes and moan. I. Can. Not. Be. Lieve. It.

Did I taste a hint of finely grated lemon rind mixed in with the soury sweetness? The cream filling is truly decadent, almost like mousse.

It's even better than the ones I tasted at the Whoopie Pie Festival in Pennsylvania a few years ago! Better than *any* I've had. Like. Ever.

No wonder Elijah wants to marry Henry! Okay, so he wouldn't if he knew they were from his best friend.

I eat half of the lemon whoopie pie and set it aside, mentally apologizing to it for my neglect and promising to come back for more. But the other ones are just staring back at me all lonely. I *have to* try another flavor.

I greedily reach toward the plate and choose my next victim. This one appears to be chocolate with peanut butter filling and...oh, my!

My eyes roll back in pure ecstasy as the perfect blend of peanut butter and chocolate hit my tastebuds. Instead of the typical cake batter for the outside, it tastes like Henry used a brownie batter complete with melted chocolate chips. And it's nothing short of amazing.

Jah, I think Henry Yoder missed his calling. Because I know for a fact that he could win *any* dessert baking contest anywhere with these extraordinary whoopie pies. What on earth was he doing working in construction and wasting his time building houses when he could clearly be a world-famous culinary artist?

Nee, not exactly an approved Amish profession. But still.

I hear noises outside and panic.

Then I grin like the Cheshire Cat in *Alice in Wonderland*. Not that I know exactly what that means. But I've read about it before in books, and I tend to have quite an imagination. So I'm told. We were never allowed to read *Alice in Wonderland* growing up, but I never questioned why.

Before anyone comes back in to steal my edible treasures, I toss the foil back on the plate of whoopie pies and dash upstairs to stash them in my room. Because there is *no* way I'm going to share these delicious morsels from Heaven with anyone. I'm mourning the fact that I allowed Eli to snatch a few earlier. *Ach, vell.* Guess I can't be too stingy.

How on earth did Henry Yoder manage to make *the best* whoopie pies ever?

CHAPTER 5

*H*ENRY

I stare out at the frozen pond thinking tonight can't come soon enough. I wish Elijah would show up and help me ready the pond for our hockey match tonight. *Jah*, it's a little early, but I wouldn't mind practicing a bit so I can show off for Ellie.

I can't wait to see her tonight. I've thought of little else since our time together last night. I'm still stoked that I got to kiss her.

I just know that she must've loved the whoopie pies. I've been imagining her reaction to them all day, since I dropped them off on her doorstep early this morning. Maybe I'll even get another kiss.

I snort at the thought. *Jah*, right. In my dreams.

But, stranger things have happened. I don't know what they are, but I'm sure it must be true since everyone says it. And, honestly, I haven't really sat down to think about it. If I did, no doubt I could come up with something.

"Henry?"

I whirl around at my neighbor's voice. One I haven't heard in many months.

"Jude!" He strides near and we fist each other's shoulders—our masculine version of a hug. Jude's a couple inches taller than my six-foot-two frame, and I can see by his bulk he's been working out since he left the farm to play hockey for a brand-new professional team. "I hoped you'd be back in town soon. How are things going in your fancy hockey world?"

"Pretty amazing. I have a short break, so I thought I would come see my mom. She's been missing me."

"I'm sure she has." I won't mention Jude's father. It has always been a sore subject with my friend.

"Hey, how's your mom and sister?" Jude stuffs his hands in his pockets and glances toward the house.

"My mom called and said she won't be home until later. Been up in Ohio helping out with her folks. But Ivy's still here. She's taking off somewhere but is pretty tight-lipped about it."

"I imagine that if I was a girl, I wouldn't want my brother knowing all my business either." Jude chuckles. "Mind if I go say hello?"

"Nah." But I don't want Jude and Ivy to be alone, so I accompany my friend to the house.

"Are you playing on the pond tonight?" Jude's head angles toward the frozen water, eagerness in his eyes.

"That's the plan. Gonna join us and show us farm boys how to play?"

Jude laughs. "I think some of you guys can still show me a thing or two."

I shake my head. "I doubt that."

"Hey, Eli was pretty darn good if I recall correctly."

When we reach the house, the door bursts open.

"Jude!" Ivy squeals and practically bowls our neighbor over. She's always liked Jude, but I've never seen this much enthusiasm for him.

"Hey, Ives." Jude kisses her cheek, and I try not to growl. Why would he do that? "I see you've missed me."

Ivy bounces on her toes. "Did you bring us tickets?" Her grin spreads wide.

"Aw, is that all I'm good for?" He chuckles good-naturedly.

"I can bribe you with whoopie pies." Ivy holds the plate out.

"Those are for tonight, sis, but I suppose we can spare a couple for Jude," I say.

Jude snaps his fingers. "Shucks. Coach has us all on a strict diet. Otherwise..." He shrugs.

"You *have* to taste them. They are so good. Henry made them for his girlfriend." Ivy sings.

Jude eyes me. "You have a girlfriend, huh?"

I shake my head. "I wish."

Jude laughs. "Still crushing on Ellie Petersheim?"

"You know it." I can't help but smile at her name.

"Well, don't give up. She's gotta come around sooner or later, right?" I love the fact that Jude is so encouraging. He looks at Ivy. "I guess I can try a bite." He winks at her and again I stuff down my irritation.

"Take your pick. Strawberry, lemon, and chocolate peanut butter." Ivy raises her eyebrows twice.

"They all sound good." Jude snags a strawberry whoopie pie and bites into it, the filling landing square on his stubbled chin. "Oh, wow. This is amazing." He swipes his chin, takes another bite, and sets the treat down.

"Think they'll win her over?" My face stretches as I don't even attempt to contain my smile.

"If these don't, I don't know what will, bro."

I pump a fist in the air. "That's what I'm praying for."

"So, you need help clearing the pond so we can get some practice in?" Jude eyes me.

I grin. "Thought you'd never ask."

CHAPTER 6

ELLIE

"Ellie, Duke's all hitched up and ready to go. Are you coming?" Elijah calls from what sounds like the back mudroom door.

I glance down at my pink dress one last time. Hopefully, it's Henry's least favorite color. I don't think boys usually like pink, do they? But I wonder if anyone will even see my dress because I will likely keep my winter coat on the entire time we're outside. And Henry's barn isn't usually much warmer.

"Ellie, let's go now. Or I'm leaving without you." Eli's aching to play hockey. Since the guys can only play when the pond is frozen, they try to get in as much playing time as possible in the winter. It's a special treat that the guys looked forward to, then mourn when the ice melts.

I grab the bag of chips and salsa we're contributing to the snack table tonight, then rush to the door. "You're so impatient, *bruder*." I say as I plop my traveling bonnet over my prayer *kapp*.

"I'm not impatient. I just told Henry I would go a little early and help him clear the pond and separate the men's and women's sides."

"Not all the guys like to play hockey. Some just like to skate." I point out as I hop up into Elijah's courting buggy.

"True." He rolls his eyes as he signals to Duke. "You know what I mean. Separate the ice skaters from the hockey players. Whatever."

I eye my brother curiously. "So, did you know Henry was going to steal Simon's buggy and trick me into riding with him last night?"

Eli squirms in his seat but says nothing.

I point at his face. "Ah ha! You did know. Why didn't you warn me?"

"You know how long Henry's been wanting to court you, Ellie. How else was the poor guy going to get a break? He did ask first, you know. He's asked many times."

I cross my arms over my chest. "And I said no."

"*Jah*, you *always* say no." Eli shakes his head. "I don't know what it is with you, Ellie."

My face flushes at his accusation. My brother thinks I'm being unreasonable!

"Henry's a good guy. He deserves a chance, don't you think?"

"Right. Like a good guy would deceive a girl into a buggy ride."

Eli frowns. "What else is he supposed to do? Wait around until you're married off to someone else? I feel sorry for him."

Why is Elijah being so insistent about Henry? "And you don't feel sorry for Simon?"

Eli sneers. "A guy who's willing to be paid off isn't marriage material, Ellie."

Honestly, marrying Simon has never even crossed my mind. I feel my eyes widening. "Paid off?"

"*Jah*. Your little buggy ride last night cost Henry a hundred dollars."

Maybe this should flatter me, but instead it offends me. "I'm not a head of cattle that can just be sold off to the highest bidder!"

"Simon wanted new speakers for his buggy." Eli shrugs as though speakers are a logical reason to pull the carpet out from under me.

Boys! "It just figures that Henry Yoder would do something so...so...barbaric!"

"Why aren't you blaming Simon? He's the one who sold you out. Henry just wants to be with you. You can't fault a man for doing everything he can to get his girl."

"I. Am. Not. His. Girl." I grind out the words.

"So you've said." Elijah's eyebrows lift and his grin broadens, and I just *know* I'm not going to like his next comment. "Did you kiss him?"

"I...I..." I sputter. "*Ach*, it's none of your business."

Eli has the audacity to laugh. "Must've been some kiss."

If he only knew. But I refute it anyhow. Or, at least, I try to.

"I didn't say we kissed!" I know my cheeks must be a thousand shades of red right now, because I'm suddenly hot.

"You didn't have to, sis. I can see it all over your face. Plus, you aren't denying it. If you and Henry *didn't* kiss, you would have just said no." Eli shakes his head. "So, you *do* secretly like Henry."

"I do not!" I huff. "And he kissed me without my permission."

"He *what*?" Oh, no. Elijah's hands tighten on the reins as we turn into the Yoders' property.

I didn't mean to rile up my brother's protective side. I need to backpedal. And fast. "Elijah—"

He stops Duke in front of the hitching post and turns to me, eyes intent on mine. A muscle clenches in his jaw. "Ellie, if he forced you…"

"Elijah, it wasn't like that. Calm down."

Eli jumps from the carriage. "But you said he kissed you without permission. And my *schweschder* is not a liar. Don't try to defend him."

Oh, goodness. Now, what have I done?

My mouth goes dry as Henry approaches us, his smile wide. Wow, he looks even better today. If that's possible. So much for avoiding Henry.

No, Ellie. No, he does not *look good. Well, I mean, let's be honest, he* does, *but he's not for you.* I try to strengthen my resolve but it's a challenge. Not gonna lie.

"Pretty in pink," are the words that issue from Henry's perfect mouth in a low rumble. So much for trying to guess his least favorite color. It figures.

Of course, I could probably wear a potato sack and Henry would find something positive to say.

Then his gaze snags mine and tangles. And, goodness, I can't look away.

Until Elijah gives Henry a hard shove, pulling us both out of our stupor.

"Elijah!" What has gotten into him?

Henry rights himself and stares at his best friend. "Hey! What was that for?"

"For kissing my sister without her permission." Eli's fists clench.

Henry's gaze falls on me again, a look of shock and yet pleasure encompassing his features. "You told your brother about our kiss?"

The way his tone gentles does something to my insides. It's like a caress from his lips to my soul.

I need to get away from Henry as soon as humanly possible because this is *not* how tonight is supposed to play out. I'm supposed to be avoiding him. Not discussing how *wunderbaar* our kiss was.

I turn and scurry to the house. Once I'm safely inside, I realize I forgot the chips and salsa in the buggy. And I just know Henry will think I left them on purpose just to get another look at him.

And he may not be entirely wrong.

CHAPTER 7

ENRY

I saw a spark of hope. It was a tiny spark, but still.

Now, I'm more determined than ever to win Ellie over. When our eyes collided tonight, I knew in that moment that a relationship with Ellie was not a lost cause. I just need to be patient and stay the course.

I still can't believe she shared our most intimate moment with her brother. *Jah*, he's my best friend, but for her to admit that we kissed? That's huge. And I haven't even asked her about the whoopie pies yet.

"You're not doing that again." Eli's words pull me from my musings.

"How's that?"

"Ellie. I don't want you ever kissing her without

her permission first." His glare is one I've rarely seen. Elijah Petersheim is always the cool, calm, and collected one. "Or else you'll answer to me."

My back stiffens at the threat in his words. Surely Elijah knows he doesn't have to protect his sister from me. "She did kiss me back. And I wouldn't have gone in for the kiss if I hadn't seen the same longing in *her* eyes."

Elijah stares at me as though I've just been dropped off by a spaceship from another planet. "She kissed you back? *My schweschder* kissed *you* back? Ellie did?"

I nod and chuckle at his look of utter bewilderment. "And if I'm not mistaken, she enjoyed it too. Maybe not as much as I did, but she...*jah.*" I can't help but smile as I remember.

"But she hates you. *Mamm* said she dumped your plate of whoopie pies in the trash."

My jaw drops open at Eli's words. She threw my whoopie pies away? Yikes. I rub my chest and clench my heart. That hurts more than the bruises I have on my back from last night.

"By the way, I don't want to marry you." Elijah deadpans.

I twist my lips and take a step back. "Excuse me?"

Eli laughs now. "I told Ellie that I wanted to marry whichever of her friends made her the whoopie pies. Seeing it was you and all…" He shrugs. "Well, that's a no go. I take my words back. Deal's off."

I step close and squeeze my friend's shoulder, grateful the tension between us has cleared. "Sorry to disappoint you, bro. But I kind of have a thing for your sister."

Elijah shoves me away and guffaws. "You don't say?"

"And even if I didn't…just, no. But she really, truly tossed out my whoopie pies?" I swallow. I'm not usually emotional, but this wound cuts deep.

"*Mamm* snatched them out of the trash, though, and I may have tried one or two or five. That's how I know how good they are. And if it's any consolation, after I bragged on you—I mean, I didn't know it was *you*—but after I said I wanted to marry you, the whoopie pies mysteriously disappeared." His eyebrows lift and a look moves over his features as if he just discovered the eighth wonder.

"Maybe she threw them back in the trash." I frown.

"I don't think so." Eli shakes his head then leans close and whispers. "Between you and me, I think Ellie is harboring them in her room and secretly devouring them at will."

My hope soars. "So, you think she actually tried them?"

"That would be my guess."

Jude approaches us with his hockey duffle on his arm. He lifts it up. "Coach Graves made me promise that if I play on the pond, I must use my gear. He doesn't want any injuries."

Maybe a little overkill, but hey, I don't play professional hockey so what would I know?

Jude looks between us. "What were you two whispering about over here?"

"He wants to marry me." I tease. I don't think I'll ever let Elijah live that one down.

"Say what?" Jude's eyes widen.

"Just ignore him." Eli bats the air. "Actually, did you know our friend Henry here is an expert in the kitchen? You should see him with his pink apron on."

"Really?" Jude eyes me.

"He liked my whoopie pies. That's why he wants to marry me. My pink apron notwithstanding." I laugh.

"Those whoopie pies *were* good." Jude agrees. "But a marriage proposal? I don't know about that."

"I'm trying to woo Ellie, not her brother." I clarify.

"Alright, that's enough." Red faced, Elijah turns and walks off toward the barn.

"I think you might've offended him." Jude watches Eli retreat inside through the barn door.

"Nah, he'll get over it. Probably going to seek out more whoopie pies." I laugh. "Do you have any advice for me about Ellie?"

"Yeah. Don't give up. It sounds like you're on the right track." He scratches his stubbled cheek. "But between you and me, you might want to keep Elijah away from your whoopie pies."

At Jude's comment, we both laugh.

Then I point to the pond. "Should we put our skates on and get some practice in?"

"Now you're speaking *my* love language." Jude chuckles.

CHAPTER 8

*E*LLIE

"Between you and me," Henry's sister, Ivy, says as she hefts a backpack over her shoulder, "I think you should just date Henry. I mean, why not? It's not like you're agreeing to marry him or anything."

I frown. "But that would be leading him on. And it wouldn't be fair to either of us."

"Well, suit yourself. But you'll never find a man more devoted to you than Henry is. Trust me, I've looked."

I think about the conversation my brother Elijah and I had earlier. How he said Simon had sold me out for a radio or speakers or whatever. And then I think about Henry, who not only paid a hundred dollars to take me home but made me whoopie pies. A place deep inside me warms at the thought, though I don't want to admit it.

As though reading my mind, Ivy adds, "He was up until three o'clock baking whoopie pies. I don't think he even got any sleep."

I glance out the window just in time to see Henry lift his hand to his mouth to cover a yawn. It *is* a sweet gesture—no pun intended—even for Henry. But does it make up for all the past wrongs he's done?

As much as I'm tempted to let my guard down, I can't. I don't trust Henry Yoder. Plain and simple.

"What is it about Henry you don't like? That's what I've always wondered."

Do I dare pour my heart out to Ivy? Let my guard down? "Do you promise to keep this between us?"

Ivy frowns. "Now you have me worried. Did my brother do something to you?"

I sigh. "Maybe not the way you're thinking, but *jah*. He hurt me."

"What did he do?" Concern floods Ivy's features.

"I mean, when I say it out loud to someone else, it sounds kind of *dumm*. Petty even. But, I have my reasons."

"I won't judge you, Ellie."

I take a deep breath. "When I was in fourth grade,

Henry stole my lunch. And I know it doesn't sound like a big deal, but to me it was huge." Should I expound? "You know my family has never been well off. And my *schweschder* was having a lot of health problems around that time. *Mamm* and *Dat* tried to hide it, but our family was struggling. Well, *Mamm* let me take the last of what we had for my lunch that day."

I laugh bitterly then continue. "It was a peanut butter and jelly sandwich, chips, an apple, and a whoopie pie for dessert. It was probably the largest lunch I'd ever had, but *Mamm* insisted. So, I took it, dreaming of lunchtime all morning." I couldn't help the tears in my eyes.

I wouldn't mention that later that day I saw Henry behind the schoolhouse showing interest in one of my friends. It was the last straw. I may have been a teensy bit jealous.

"And Henry ate it?" Ivy's tone was gentle.

"All of it." I nod.

"I'm so sorry, Ellie. But you know boys that age don't have many brains. And I'm sure he wouldn't have stolen your lunch if he knew about your situation." Ivy shakes her head. "It sounds like I'm making excuses for him, but there is no excuse for bad behavior. Henry shouldn't have done that. No doubt."

Ivy continues. "But you have to know that is not

who Henry is anymore. He's a man now, and probably more mature than most young men his age. I think our dad's passing had a lot to do with that. It's made him sensitive and built his character."

"I think I might be starting to realize that."

Ivy turns serious. "Do you want me to make him apologize?"

"I'm not sure he even remembers, honestly."

"And you can't forget it." Ivy squeezes my hand and her eyes hold sympathy.

"Seems that way."

"Maybe you should consider forgiving him, *ain't so*? It would be less of a burden on your shoulders. And by the sound of your family situation, you have plenty of that."

Isn't that the truth? "*Jah*, you're probably right."

A car's honk sounds from outside. Ivy glances toward the door.

"Well, I should be going. My ride is waiting for me." She smiles now. "It was good talking with you, Ellie. And maybe, just give Henry a second chance."

"I'll think about it."

"Pray about it too. You never know what God might have planned." Ivy says goodbye, then disappears out the door.

Henry must've made several batches of whoopie

pies because two platefuls sit on the Yoders' kitchen table. Just then, I realize I'm alone in Henry's house.

I glance out the window at the pond to see what looks like the three guys already working up a sweat. I notice Henry and Eli by their beanies, and Henry's neighbor Jude by all his hockey gear—a helmet, pads, the whole nine yards.

It wonders me what it would be like to be an *Englischer*. Then I shiver, imagining how scary it would be out in the world where everyone is a stranger. At least here in my Amish community, I have family and friends. I've always felt sorry for the Amish folks that leave after they've become a member of the church and then face the shunning. To lose my entire community would be devastating.

But I do understand the pull of the world. To not have all these rules govern my life is appealing. I've heard stories of people not being allowed to do the simplest of things because the *Ordnung* forbids it. I couldn't imagine getting into trouble with the leaders because I have one too many straight pins on my dress. How can that be considered worldly? It just doesn't make sense to me.

It may sound funny to the *Englisch*, but for the Amish it is serious stuff.

One time, Eli was out working on our farm and he

had his hat on at an awkward angle because of the sun. The deacon happened to be driving by, stopped, and warned my brother that his hat position was worldly, and he better make sure he was wearing it properly—after all, one of the younger boys could happen by and get his own ideas about not having to follow the rules. It could lead to wearing baseball caps or a cowboy hat, and then they'd be just like the world. That might cause them to desire more of the worldly trappings, leave the Amish, and be in danger of going to hell, the deacon had reasoned.

Which got me wondering, who decides whether something is worldly or not? And does the deacon believe that everyone who isn't Amish—or anyone who leaves the Amish, for that matter—is doomed to hell? Even if the deacon believes it, I don't. Because I don't ever recall one Bible verse that has the word Amish in it. I even looked it up on one of the library computers one time, but I couldn't find it anywhere. If that is what is required for salvation, wouldn't God want the world to know?

But the more I think about it and the more I read my Bible, I think maybe the leaders don't have every-thing right. Like, why would the Bible say that man looks on the outside, but God looks on the heart? It's pretty clear to me that God sees things differently than we do.

And didn't God say that a person is *not* made right with God by the works he does? Only faith in Jesus can make people right with God, is what I understood when *Dat* read the verses in the Bible. *For by grace are ye saved through faith; and that not of yourselves: it is the gift of God: not of works, lest any man should boast.* It seems pretty clear to me.

I sigh and realize that I might be here for a while. Alone in Henry's house. I'm overcome with the urge to sneak around. Not that I've never been here before. I've attended church in the Yoders' home many times. But I've never been here alone. Until now.

It wonders me what Henry's bedroom looks like. Is it any different from Eli's? Probably. After all, both Elijah and myself have to share our rooms with our siblings. But the Yoders only have Ivy and Henry.

What would it be like to have my very own bedroom for myself? Why, I could have complete and total privacy. I could hide things if I had a notion to.

I check out the windows one more time and see the guys still playing hockey on the pond. It will be at least an hour or two before anyone else shows up, probably.

What would it hurt? I don't think the Yoders

would mind. It's not like they have anything to hide. After all, all their curtains are open. And the deacon always said that closed curtains are a sign that you're hiding something. Not that she ever gave much credence to the deacon's *ferhoodled* notions.

"Hello? Is anybody here?" I call out just in case.

When silence answers back, I grin, then make my way toward the stairs. Why am I tip-toeing? Even if it's sneaky, it's not like the mice are going to tell on me.

I turn right at the top of the steps and stop at the entrance of what is probably Ivy's room, judging by the feminine colors on the quilt. Either that, or it could belong to their *mamm*. But I'm pretty sure that Martha Yoder sleeps downstairs like my *mamm* and *dat*. It's easier to keep track of the *kinner's* whereabouts that way.

Not wanting to disturb Ivy's room, I move down the hall to find the bathroom. Of course, I already knew this was a bathroom, so I don't know why I checked. Silly me.

One thing I am thankful for in my Amish community is that we are allowed to have bathrooms inside our houses. *Dat* grew up in a much stricter neighboring Amish sect and they had to go outside to use an outhouse. I couldn't even imagine using one outside, as cold as it's been lately. Fortunately, *Dat's* folks had moved to this community, and I'm blessed by the choice they made all those years ago.

Which wonders me. Are there any choices *I'm* making that will bring blessings to future generations? I don't ponder the thought too long. After all, when will I ever get another chance to scope out Henry's house unnoticed?

I turn an about face and head in the opposite direction. But I'm met with yet another feminine looking bedroom. Not Henry's.

The room I come upon next—the last one on the second story—appears to be a sewing and craft room. Not Henry's. At least, I hope not. But at the same time, he *did* make those wunderbaar whoopie pies, so...

Apparently, the women own the entire upstairs. Must be nice.

I hear a noise and stop. I listen carefully, but all is quiet again. Must've just been a squeaky board under my foot. I peek out the upstairs window just to be sure the guys are still occupied. I blow out a breath, relieved to see that they are.

I charge down the stairs in search of another bedroom.

I know the moment I open the door which bedroom is Henry's. The scent of the cologne he was wearing on our buggy ride last night lingers in the air. The scent I can't seem to forget no matter how hard I try. Not that it's an unpleasant fragrance or anything. It's just that every time I smell it, I think about kissing Henry.

And that's dangerous.

I stop at the threshold, second-guessing myself. Something about entering Henry's bedroom feels awfully intimate. I breathe in deep to fortify myself, then step inside his forbidden private sanctuary.

Like Elijah's bedroom, a rack with a shotgun hangs on the wall, along with a set of deer antlers. I suppose it's a pretty common thing in Amish young men's bedrooms. A blue chenille bedspread that matches his curtains covers his bed, but I stop myself from gliding my hand over it.

I step next to a bureau, and stare at it for several seconds. I don't want to run across Henry's under-wear, so I decide not to open the drawers. That would just be too awkward.

My eyes search the room. His closet is open, but appears rather ordinary. Henry seems to be neat and tidy for the most part. Not a bad quality in a man.

Not that I'm in the market. Especially not for Henry.

I spy a cowboy hat on one of his deer racks and

can't help myself from snatching it off the wall. *Jah*, this was the same kind of hat the deacon warned my brother to avoid lest he be in danger of hellfire. Apparently, the deacon has never had the same discussion with Henry.

I search his dresser top for a mirror but find none, so I open his desk drawer. My eyes snag on something. A journal?

I lift it out and several pictures slide into my hands. I swallow as my likeness stares back at me. When did Henry take this? And how? That's when I realize that Henry is in the picture too off in the distance. Maybe his *Englisch* neighbor, Jude, took these with his phone. *Jah*, that made sense.

Something about Henry owning a photo of me warms my insides. It wonders me how often he looks at it. Is it a daily ritual or something he does occasionally or not at all?

I take another look at myself in the photo. Probably not the cutest I've ever looked, but I suppose I look alright. At least I wasn't in the middle of talking or eating. Because that would be embarrassing if my mouth was all crooked or I had a giant green salad leaf on one of my front teeth.

I banish the thought, sift through a few more photos, and finally slide them back into the notebook.

I'm about to close it when I catch a handwritten phrase amongst the pages of Henry's journal.

I never meant for it to happen.

Ach, did Henry write this? What did he not mean to happen?

I turn to the first page and begin reading.

Dear Dad,

That's all the writing on the first page. Several random dried splotches fill the remainder of the paper. My heart clenches as I realize that Henry must've been crying when he wrote those words. Perhaps continuing his thoughts had been too painful?

Whatever it was, my heart went out to him. Poor, Henry.

I read page after page as Henry pours out his heart to his father. My tears can't be stopped, although I do my best to brush them away. It is the single most heart-breaking thing I've ever read. I never realized how much Henry suffered after his father's death.

Maybe Ivy was right. Maybe I don't know Henry, the man.

I hear footsteps and swipe away the remainder of my tears.

But before I have time to escape or even think, I spin around. "Henry!" I say breathless, as he steps into his bedroom.

His grin broadens when he sees me and appears to drink me in. "Oh, heck, yes!"

I realize that I'm still wearing his cowboy hat. And apparently, he likes me in it.

And then I realized the drawer behind me is still open. Oh, no! Henry cannot know that I've been snooping through his most personal thoughts. He can't.

I may not want Henry to court me, but I'm not a monster. And I just did a monster thing. I chide myself for being so intrusive and not minding my own business.

His brow furrows and his eyes begin roaming the bedroom. He *cannot* find out what I've been doing—what I've been reading.

I utter a silent prayer for a distraction of some sort.

"What are you..." His voice trails off as he steps near and I know that if he comes any closer, he will figure it out.

And I can't just close the drawer without him noticing.

I'm desperate, so I do what any sane woman would do. I grab the front of Henry's shirt, ignoring his wide eyes, and yank him down to my lips. But I completely miss his mouth and kiss the side of his nose.

Until he pulls me flush against him and claims my

mouth like his life depends on it. His eager hands roam my back, and I have to suppress a whimper. Because, goodness, I could get addicted to Henry's touch.

The cowboy hat falls to the floor, forgotten.

As much as I don't like Henry, I realize that I love his kisses.

I almost forget my mission, but I can't seem to pry my hands off his chest to reach back and push the drawer closed. So, instead I lift my foot behind me and move to shut the drawer I'd just been snooping through. But somehow the low heel of my boot gets caught on something. I try to yank it away, but in the process, the force of my propulsion sends both Henry and me onto his bed.

"Ellie," he groans.

Oh, goodness. Now, what have I done?

At first, I worry that I've accidentally kneed him between the legs. Until he tilts his head and deepens the kiss. Then I know it isn't a groan of pain, but of passion. And goodness gracious, Henry Yoder *knows* how to kiss!

Can we just stay like this forever?

Apparently not because not a moment later, another voice captures our attention. A feminine voice. Henry's *mother's* voice. *Ach.*

Jumpin' Jehosaphat! We're in trouble.

Eli and Jude choose that moment to appear in the doorway next to Henry's *mamm*. All three of them stand gaping at us with bewildered expressions.

Henry and I both bolt upright, consequently banging our foreheads together.

And that's when I'm struck by the fact that there is no way on earth I will be able to convince Henry Yoder —or anyone else—that I don't like him.

And if I admit it to myself, I kinda do.

But I'm not about to admit it to myself or anyone else. Ever.

CHAPTER 9

H*ENRY*

I'm not sure what prompted Ellie to kiss me like that, but I'm *not* going to complain.

Even if *Mamm* grabbed my arm, hauled me out into the mudroom, and is glaring at me like she's about to send me out into the yard for a tree branch. "Henry Clarence Yoder!"

Three names. I'm in trouble.

"What in the world possessed you to take advantage of sweet Ellie Petersheim? This is not the behavior I expect to see from you while I'm out caring for your grandparents, young man. I should...I should ground you!"

I try to picture my five-foot-four mother disciplining me. I can't help it. I attempt to hold in a laugh, but it bursts forth anyhow.

I'm so floored from Ellie's kiss right now, I don't think *anything* can dampen my mood.

"This isn't funny! How am I going to explain this to Ellie's mother?" I hear stress in *Mamm's* voice and realize I need to de-escalate this situation as soon as possible.

"Mom. You don't need to say *anything* to Ellie's mother. Or anybody else. It's none of their business."

"You don't think Ellie's mother has a right to know that my son and her daughter were caught..." She waves her hand haphazardly.

"Making out." I finish the sentence for her since she didn't seem to want to describe what she walked in on. Something I will be dreaming about as I lay my head on my pillow tonight, no doubt. And that I'll be daydreaming about every waking hour.

Really, I can't get over how amazing—and quite unexpected—that was. Just to find her in my room wearing my cowboy hat had me reeling with delight. She looked so irresistibly cute. But to have her lips on mine? Her hand clutching my chest? Her fingers in my hair? Of her own volition? Priceless.

"How am I supposed to leave again, knowing you're bringing women into your bedroom?"

"It wasn't like that, *Mamm*. And that's the first time Ellie, or any woman besides you and Ivy for that matter, has ever been in my bedroom. You don't need to worry about me. I'll be fine." I need to change the subject. "When are you going back to Ohio? How's *grossdawdi*?"

Tears glaze *Mamm's* eyes. "He's taken a turn for the worse. I didn't plan on going back this soon, but I need to be there. Since your *grossmammi* has dementia, hospice has come to help out. They're staying at the house until I get back tonight. The driver's still waiting outside."

"Tonight? You're not even staying the night here?"

"That's what I was coming into your room to tell you, son." *Mamm* glances around. "Where's Ivy? I didn't see her."

The last thing I want to do is burden *Mamm* any further. "She's not here right now. Was there something you wanted to tell her?"

"When is she coming back?"

"I don't know. I think it's going to be awhile." My description isn't detailed, but it's also not a lie. *You're welcome, Ivy.* Besides, if *Mamm's* not going to be here anyway, Ivy's absence will be less for her to worry about.

Mamm sighs. "I was hoping to see her too, but I

guess it'll have to be next time. Are things going well here, then?"

"Things are fine, *Mamm*. Don't worry about anything here."

"Well, okay. If you're sure."

"I'm sure. If Ivy or I need anything, we'll call. You need to get some rest yourself too, *Mamm*. Don't wear yourself ragged. We still need you."

Mamm pats my cheek. "You're such a good son. So much like your father."

At *Mamm's* words, I almost tear up. I always looked up to my father when he was alive. And now that I'm the man in charge of the family, I think I appreciate him even more. I never realized how much *dat* did for all of us. "*Denki.*"

Then I watch *Mamm* as she heads toward the waiting vehicle with an overnight bag over her shoulder. If I would have thought about it, I should have carried it out to the car for her. But it's too late now.

With Ivy and *Mamm* both gone, it'll be lonely for the next couple of nights. The kind of nights that will have me wishing I had a *fraa* to share them with.

My mind immediately goes back to my time in the bedroom with Ellie and a wave of heat surges through me. Then I smile thinking of my possible future. *Our* future.

CHAPTER 10

ELLIE

"Do you want to tell me what *that* was all about?" I'm still sitting on Henry's bed as Elijah taps an inpatient foot on the floor, a scowl hardening his face.

Henry's cowboy hat is lying next to my brother's dancing boot, as though they're together at a dance hall.

Jude looks back and forth between us, then mercifully, makes a beeline for the kitchen.

I watch him go, then shrug. "Not really."

"I thought you didn't like Henry Yoder." His eyes squint, as though he's examining my every thought.

"I don't. Not really." At least, I never *thought* I did.

"Then why in the world did I just see you practically *on top* of him with your lips glued together?"

I wince at Elijah's words. Because not only did he and Jude just see that unintended fiasco, Henry's *mamm* did too. My cheeks burn at the embarrassing thought.

That's a good question. One I'm still trying to figure out myself.

Instead of answering, I shrug again. Because I can't just say that I was snooping through Henry's personal belongings, and I didn't want to get caught so I concocted a last-second scheme to distract him. Of course, the original distraction didn't include Henry's bed, but here we are. Or there we were. Whatever.

"Do I need to have another talk with Henry? Did he force himself on you, Ellie?" Elijah stands like he's prepared for battle, his fists tightened.

The last thing I want to do is ruin their friendship. "What? *Nee.*"

He visibly relaxes and his hands unclench. He unloads a sigh. "Ellie. I don't know what to make of this. You're not making any sense. Either you like Henry or you don't."

"I...*don't?*" Honestly, I'm a little confused myself. Because the more I discover about Henry, the more I *do* like. Is it possible I've been wrong about him all this time?

"Do you want me to tell Henry to stay away from you?"

And now I feel sorry for the guy. Henry has every right to be in his own bedroom. I'm the interloper here. He can't help it if I attack him the moment he walks in.

"*Nee*. No, I'll deal with Henry."

Eli studies me carefully. "You're sure and certain?"

"*Jah*, I'm sure and certain."

CHAPTER 11

H*ENRY*

"So, you and Ellie Petersheim, huh?" As we lace up our hockey skates, Jude's knowing smile collides with mine. The one I haven't been able to erase since I walked into my bedroom and saw Ellie wearing my *verboten* cowboy hat. Something about that image drives me wild.

"*Jah*. Finally." At least, I hope that's what that spectacular kiss meant. If not, I'm really confused. But it wouldn't be the first time Ellie has left me confused. The woman can be a walking contradiction.

"I guess the whoopie pies must've done it then. I might need to get that recipe from you for the next time I want to impress a woman."

"Sure. No problem."

Jude looks toward the house, where Eli has just stepped outside. "Eli didn't look too happy about you and Ellie."

"I probably wouldn't be either if I saw Ivy making out with some guy in his bedroom. I, uh, wasn't expecting that. And I couldn't have planned it if I tried." I shake my head. "I still think I might have dreamed it all up."

"Oh, believe me, you weren't dreaming. You've got witnesses to prove it." Jude shakes his head in amusement.

Eli comes near, a scowl on his face. "What are you two yakking about?"

My gaze shoots to Jude, pleading.

"Dreams." Jude says, then drops the puck. He holds up his hockey stick. "Let's play!" He glides out onto the ice.

I follow our *Englisch* friend as Eli is donning his ice skates near the edge of the pond. "Thanks for the save, Jude."

"Any time." Jude passes the puck my way. "But the way Eli looks, I wouldn't be surprised if he has it out with you tonight."

"I've never seen him like this. He's livid." I skate around Jude, but he swipes the puck from my path and skates toward the opposite goal. "Besides, we don't believe in violence."

"Ah, just give him time. He'll get over it." Jude flicks his hockey stick and the puck goes sailing into the unmanned goal.

"I hope so." Jude slides the puck my way and I skate and shoot, making a goal. Not exactly a difficult thing to do when no one is defending it.

I fetch the puck out of the net, then hit it to Jude as I skate out into the middle of the pond. Eli intercepts and heads my way, the puck tucked safely next to his stick. He's still aways off from the goal but deftly swings his hockey stick. Then I realize Eli isn't aiming for the goal.

He's aiming for *me*.

The puck pings me squarely in the chest. Hard.

I tilt my head and frown at Eli. "What was that about?"

He ignores my question and skates around me in a circle, bumping my shoulder in the process.

I come to a complete stop and stare at my friend. "What the heck, Eli?"

Jude skates up to us, then comes to an abrupt halt, spraying ice everywhere in the process. "Everything okay here?" He cups Elijah's shoulder.

Eli gives me the evil eye, and I honestly don't know

what's gotten into him. I'm guessing it has to do with Ellie, but he was the one who suggested the whole buggy ride scheme. And I can't exactly apologize for kissing Ellie, because I would be lying. I'm not sorry at all. And to be frank, I hope I can get her alone again before the night ends.

"I think Eli's upset with me." I state the obvious.

"You *think*?" Eli's fists clench.

"Honestly, Eli, I don't know what you want from me. I thought you were all for me and Ellie being together. Now, I'm not so sure."

"*Jah*, well, I'm not so sure either."

He's not so sure? *Great.*

Eli glances toward the house where Ellie and some of the other *youngies*, who've arrived while we've been out on the ice, walk toward our direction with skates in hand.

My heart swells at the sight of Ellie. She's the most beautiful woman I've ever seen. And now that we've kissed—*really* kissed, well, let's just say I can't get her off my mind. Nor do I have any desire to. As a matter of fact, I wouldn't mind tossing my hockey stick and ice skates to the side and spending the rest of the evening with her. But, somehow, I don't think Elijah would go for that.

Jude looks back and forth between us. "Do you

two want to talk about this or do you want to play? It looks like some of the other guys have arrived." His chin juts toward the house.

"Let's just play." Eli says, then skates off in the opposite direction.

I sigh.

Jude looks at me and shrugs. "Can't blame a guy for wanting to protect his sister."

"*Jah*, but she doesn't need protection from me." I insist. Because I'd never do anything to hurt Ellie.

"You sure about that?" Jude's eyebrow arches.

"Yes."

Jude glances toward where Eli skates. A few of the other guys are also lacing up their ice skates. "He'll get over it."

"I hope so."

"You might want to chill for a while, though. You know, stay away from Ellie until Eli calms down."

That's the last thing I want. Especially after Ellie and I have finally made a connection. I feel like a wall has been broken down between us. I need to talk to her tonight before she leaves, because I'm hoping we can come to some kind of understanding. I'm hoping she'll let me court her now that things have happened between us.

CHAPTER 12

ELLIE

As I rearrange the snacks on the table in Henry's barn, I realize something.

I am in So. Much. Trouble.

Because those lips I tried to convince myself weren't kissable? They actually are. So kissable.

Now, I can't even look at Henry Yoder without thinking of his kissable lips.

How am I supposed to carry on like a perfectly normal person?

"Ellie."

My breath hitches at the familiar male voice calling from behind, and my toes are curling inside my boots.

I've disdained Henry for so long it seems weird to just have a normal conversation with him. Even though

I made out with him. In his bedroom. In front of witnesses. *Ach*, my face burns at the thought. What was I thinking? I wasn't thinking. Or maybe I was thinking too much. Either way, here we are.

"Can we go someplace private?" His low voice rumbles in my ear.

I swallow. Private? He wants to go someplace private. My heart is beating wildly and I suck in a fortifying breath, because someplace *private* with Henry sounds dangerous. And for some reason, I think I might want *dangerous*.

"To talk?" Henry adds.

Jah, talk. Exactly what I was thinking. "Um—"

"Stay away from my *schweschder*." Eli walks up behind Henry, practically growling.

I don't know what is going on with my brother, but he hasn't been himself tonight. Every time he skated past Henry, he trash talked or did something underhanded. I'm not sure what has gotten into him, but I've never seen him act this way before.

"Elijah, it's okay." I say.

"You aren't going anywhere with *him*, Ellie. We're leaving now. Get in the buggy."

I want to protest. Because even though I have no idea what I would say to Henry at this point, I kind of want to hear him out. But I know *Mamm* and *Dat* would disapprove if I went against Elijah's wishes.

So, instead of protesting or going someplace private with kissable-lips guy, I apologetically shrug at Henry, then I walk toward the buggy with my older brother.

I won't think about the disappointment I see in Henry's eyes.

I won't think about how his shoulders immediately droop.

And I certainly won't think about what might have happened in *private* had my *bruder* not interfered.

CHAPTER 13

ELLIE

I toss and turn in bed, my mind spinning.

I can't stop thinking about what Henry might've wanted to say to me. Was he going to ask me to go on a date with him? Did he plan to ask me what I was doing in his bedroom in the first place? Did he want to relive our kisses? I'm not certain I would have had the willpower to resist if Henry had planned to share his lips with mine... How I wish we could have talked to each other.

If only Eli hadn't gotten so riled up.

Why is Elijah acting so *ferhoodled* tonight? It isn't like my brother to be so brash. And I've *never* seen him angry with Henry before. Henry has been his best friend forever. Is he truly that upset about finding us kissing? Silly me, I thought he'd be thrilled that we were actually together. Well, not *together*, together. But after all the times Eli has suggested I give Henry a chance, I can't imagine why he would act in such a way. So, what is his problem?

I sit up in bed and slowly slip out from under the covers, trying not to wake my sisters, Anna and baby Emma, whom I share a room with. I'm clearly not going to be able to fall asleep. I may as well do some hand sewing. I tiptoe to my desk, ready to light the wick on my lamp.

A creak sounds from the floorboard outside my door.

Is someone sneaking out of the house? Elijah, perhaps? Does he have a secret girlfriend he's sneaking off to see? I know he has taken Betsy Mast home a couple times, but he doesn't seem to me to be all that serious about the relationship.

Taking care to avoid every creaky spot in the floor that has divulged my sleuthing in the past, I tiptoe to the door and open it just a crack.

Elijah's eyes widen the second he sees me. His finger flies to his lips in a hushing gesture, his eyes demanding I obey the order. He points to the staircase.

What can he possibly be doing?

I nod and follow him, careful to tiptoe around the squeaky floorboard that betrayed him. He reaches the top of the steps and pauses. *Is he listening to make sure no one is awake before going downstairs?*

I open my mouth to ask, but he shakes his head and cups a hand around his ear. Again, he points downstairs.

I crouch down beside him, stilling my thoughts and tuning my ear to the quiet voices downstairs.

"*Ach*, I just don't know, Naomi." It is *Dat*'s voice, and it sounds strained.

"*Gott* will carry us through," *Mamm* said this time.

"I know He will. I know. But what should we do about Ben's offer?"

I glance at Elijah. Could *Dat* be talking about our neighbor? "Ben Troyer?" I mouth silently.

Elijah nods.

Dat continues. "I don't want to give up more of our pastureland, but I don't know what else to do. We can sell the ten acres, and our cows will be alright. We won't have to downsize the herd like last time. The ten we have left will be enough for them. You know raising cattle has always been my dream. My legacy. I hate to give it up altogether."

My eyes widen in shock. Is our situation that bad?

We have to sell more land? My father already sold twenty acres to Ben Troyer last year, but he had said that would be enough to pay all the medical bills and get back on our feet. Had he lied about that? Or had he hoped that the money would be enough and been wrong?

Elijah props his elbows on his knees and clasps his fingers together. His knuckles turn white at the tight grip as he rests his forehead on his hands. He closes his eyes, listening close.

My pulse quickens at the evidence of Elijah's stress. What will we do?

"Is Elijah's money not enough to help with the medical bills?" *Mamm* asked.

"It helps, *jah*, it does. But not enough. And Isaac still has a few years yet before they'd hire him at the factory."

A muscle twitches in Elijah's forehead and he turns his face toward the wall away from me, but not before I see the color drain from his expression. I know *Dat's* words are devastating to him. Elijah quit the job he loved, working construction with Henry, six months ago. I suspect he took the job at the RV factory where *Dat* works to help out with the family finances. The construction work just didn't pay as much or give Elijah as many hours as the factory.

But that sacrifice wasn't enough.

Poor Elijah.

My mind scrambles for ideas to help. Maybe I can make more of my sewing creations to take to Trinkets and Treasures, the little boutique in town that allows me to consign my handicrafts. I can possibly add aprons or potholders or placemats or whatever else the owner, Missy, thinks might sell well to the tourists. Perhaps I can learn to crochet. I know there are books at the library that can teach me.

Or...or maybe I can get a job at the boutique. That's it! Surely Missy would hire me on! It wouldn't bring in much, but it could help. And maybe I can clean houses for some *Englischers* too. That's what Simon said his sister does to earn extra cash. If the *Englischers* live close enough, I can take my horse and won't have to spend any of my money on a driver.

"Maybe giving up the house would be best, then." *Mamm's* sigh is barely audible.

At *Mamm's* words, my blood runs cold. *What?* My gaze darts to Elijah, whose head swivels toward me. His shocked brown eyes mirror my own.

"*Ach*, Naomi. I don't think I can sell my *mamm* and *dat's* house." Even from all the way up the stairs, I can hear the pain in my father's voice. Tears spring to my own eyes at the thought. How can *Mamm* even suggest giving up our home?

"I know, *schatzi.*" *Mamm*'s tone is gentle, calming. "It would be hard. But we could be free of the second mortgage, at least. If we were to buy the Millers' old place, we could start fresh. It wouldn't be so bad."

My nose wrinkles. Is my mother *ferhoodled*? I can't imagine anyone, much less our family of eleven, living in that old rundown house. The place has been abandoned for the past ten years, since Ivan and Shelva Miller passed away and all their children moved out of state. I think I may have heard tell that the acreage is being leased to another member of the community for farmland, but other than that, the house and property surrounding it have remained untouched. I can't even begin to guess how much work the place will need just to be livable.

And what else did *Mamm* say? A *second* mortgage? What is a second mortgage exactly? I'll need to ask Elijah later when I get the chance.

I glance back at my brother. His face is so twisted it looks like he might be sick. I reach out and touch his hand, but he pulls it away and shakes his head. He squeezes his eyes shut tightly and leans his head back to rest on the wall behind him.

The knots forming in my stomach tighten. Is this

what has Elijah so wound up lately? Did he already know about all this?

Dear God, please help my family. I don't want us to lose our home. But I know Your will is best.

A short while later, our parents retire for the evening and all becomes silent downstairs. Elijah whispers to me, "We can talk tomorrow," before sneaking back to his room. This time he remembers to step over the creaky floorboard.

I slip back into my own room. I look at my desk, but my mind is no longer focused on my sewing projects. I can't possibly concentrate enough to get anything done tonight. I crawl back into bed, taking care not to rustle the blankets. I lie still, relaxing my body into the mattress. My eyes stare at the dark ceiling above me, unseeing.

How can our situation be that bad? My heart breaks for my folks, for the pain I heard in their voices, for the burden they carry.

How can I be a help to my family in our time of need? Maybe I can contribute more money somehow. I determine here and now that I will talk to Missy about adding items to my inventory and ask her about working at the boutique. Anything I can do to help *Mamm* and *Dat*, I will.

"Elijah!" I call out to my brother the moment I spot him near the barn after work. It's the first opportunity we have had to speak since everything that transpired last night.

Elijah sighs. "What is it, Ellie?"

"I want to talk about last night."

"Say on." I won't allow his impatience to rile me up. I know he's under a lot of stress. As the second oldest male in our family, he feels almost as responsible as *Dat*.

That's why I'm glad he has hockey with the guys several evenings a week when the Yoders' pond is frozen. It's one of the ways he can relax and not think about all our burdens.

I glance around to make sure we're alone, before saying in an almost whisper, "Do you think we really might lose the house? Are things that bad?" Before he responds, I fold my arms over my chest and watch him closely. "And did you already know about all this?"

He rubs his palm over his forehead. "Yes, Ellie, I knew. About some of it anyway. I overheard a similar conversation *Dat* had over the phone at work yesterday with Ben Troyer. It sounded like Ben was trying to convince *Dat* to sell him more land. *Dat* was trying to talk him into offering a higher price." Elijah shrugs.

"And what about the house?"

Eli sighs and shakes his head. His eyes are fixed on his boots, as though he can't bear to meet my gaze. "I didn't know they are thinking about selling the house, but I did know about the second mortgage and the medical bills."

I reach out and touch his arm. "What can we do?"

His pained eyes meet mine. "I wish I knew, Ellie. I've tried everything I can think of. I thought working with *Dat* at the factory would be enough."

"I know it helps, Eli. And I'm going to see if I can work at the boutique to earn some money."

"Will *Mamm* and *Dat* let you?"

I nod, then plop down onto a bale of hay. "I talked to *Mamm* about it today. In fact, I was wondering if we could drive into town and stop at the store before we go to Henry's tomorrow night for hockey."

Elijah's eyes narrow as he brushes Duke. "I'm not certain you should be going anywhere near Henry Yoder."

"That's *enough*, Elijah. You're my brother, not *Dat*. I can be around Henry if I so choose. And besides, what do you have against him all of a sudden? I thought you *wanted* me to like him."

"Is that what's happening here? Now you *like* Henry?" Elijah crosses his arms, a smug look on his face.

"I...well, I...I don't know *how* I feel about Henry. Not exactly. But he's not a *bad* guy." I can hardly believe the words coming from my own mouth. "Besides that, he's *your* best friend. Why are you so mad at him all of a sudden?"

"I don't know, maybe because I don't know if I can trust Henry. Maybe because I saw him in a compromising position with my little sister. My sister, might I add, who has hated him for years. So, I figure either he's made passes at you before and that's why you didn't want to ride with him, or you know about something else he's done that I don't know about." He raises an eyebrow at me. "So, which is it?"

"He hasn't made any passes at me, Elijah. I mean, he did kiss me on our buggy ride, which you already know about. But, for the most part, Henry has been nothing but gentlemanly to me." *Jah*, I actually said those words. Who am I and what have I done with myself?

Well, other than when he deceived me into thinking I was going on a buggy ride with Simon, when it was Henry driving. Or when he tossed me over his shoulder in the cornfield. Or when he...I clear my thoughts with a shake of my head. Elijah doesn't need to know about *everything*. If he did, for sure and certain, he wouldn't let poor Henry within a hundred yards of me.

"If Henry's never done anything to you, then why have you always hated him?" But by Elijah's look, he isn't buying my explanation. "Help me understand."

I sigh, pulling out a long piece of straw from the bale I'm sitting on. "I know it's going to sound silly to you. But Henry stole my lunch from me when I was in fourth grade."

"What?" Elijah frowns. "That's it? *That's* what you've been so bitter about?"

"It was a special lunch, though. *Mamm* packed it for me. It had barbecue chips and an apple and everything. Even a whoopie pie."

"Oh." Eli nods. I know he understands the significance of getting such treats in a school lunch when we were *kinner*.

"I know it's silly to hold onto that memory, especially when it's been so long, but it's hard to forget." I shrug.

"*Nee*, I remember Henry back then. He wasn't always nice to be around. But he's really not like that anymore, Ellie. He's changed. Especially with his *dat* passing away a couple years ago. He's grown up."

My heart aches at the thought of Henry losing his father, remembering the heartfelt words he had poured out into his journal. For sure and certain, the loss hit him hard.

"*Jah*, I know," I answer quietly.

I stand from the hay bale and observe the gentle way Eli cares for his horse. Then I consider the way he cares for his family. He'll make a good husband and father someday.

The half-grin on Elijah's face is the first one I've seen since he took a bite of Henry's whoopie pie. "I'll tell you what, Ellie. I will smooth things out between me and Henry, if *you* can forgive him. You know the poor guy has been pining over you for years now."

For some reason, that thought doesn't irritate me like it used to. In fact, the idea of Henry Yoder pining after me actually warms my insides. I know Eli is right. I should give him a chance. And, remembering his heart-stopping kisses I can't seem to stop thinking about, I suddenly realize I might just be pining after Henry as well.

I notice Elijah's hand sticking out in front of me. I grasp it and we shake on it. "Alright, I'll do my best to forget the past." I nod and smile at my brother, glad to have cleared the air between us.

"Just no more making out in his bedroom, please."

Eli gives me a wry grin. "There's only so much a brother can witness without wanting to throw punches."

I tuck my head, a blush heating my cheeks at the memory.

"No promises, big brother." Laughing, I duck away from the stall entrance as Elijah groans and tosses a curry comb at me.

CHAPTER 14

*H*ENRY

My head jerks up the moment there's a knock on my door.

Who would be here this early in the morning? Mom should be gone for several days, if not weeks, and I don't expect Ivy back for at least another day.

I can only hope it's who I've been thinking about nonstop for the last few days. But would she be knocking on my door at this hour? Had she snuck away without anyone knowing?

My heartbeat quickens at the thought. Ellie and me. Here. At my house. All alone.

I can hardly contain myself as I swing the door open.

And my hope plummets to the floor like a lead weight.

But I recover quickly. "Eli? What are you—"

"Can we talk?" His previous ire from the other night seems to have evaporated as he stares solemnly at the ground.

"Eli? Is everything okay?" Panic seizes my heart as I run through the possibilities of what could possibly be wrong with my friend. Or, is it Ellie? "Eli? What—"

"Ellie's fine. That's not what this is about."

"Okay, then what's up?" I open the door wide. "*Kumm* inside. It's just the two of us."

He follows me into the kitchen.

I hold up a coffee mug. "Want some coffee?"

"Sure." He slouches into one of the dining chairs.

I add a couple of spoons of instant coffee grounds to each cup, then fetch water from the kettle on my stove, and pour it in.

I walk to the table and join Eli, then slide his coffee across the surface. "I've got a couple of extra whoopie pies from yesterday. Want one?"

A wry smile lifts the corner of his mouth.

"Don't worry, I'm not worried about a marriage proposal." I tease. I can't help it. I will never be able to look at a whoopie pie the same way again.

Eli groans. "You will never let me live that down, will you?"

"Probably not." I eye him. "Ready to talk about why you came over here?"

"It's kind of complicated, but I guess I'll just lay it out." His eyes glaze over. "My folks are talking about selling the farm and moving."

My pulse quickens. If Ellie and Eli move away… there's no way I'm about to let that happen. "What? Why?"

"Debt." Eli shrugs. "I guess they can't get ahead. Even with *Dat* and me both working at the factory."

"*Ach*, I'm sorry to hear that. Where would you move?" I'm almost afraid to ask.

"They're talking about buying Ivan Miller's old place."

Whew! It was still in the community. But the Millers' old place?

Eli frowns, then adds. "It's cheap."

"It's a dump." I scratch my chin. "I'm sorry. But really? I don't even know if that place would be worth fixing up."

"Right?" He sighs and takes a sip of his coffee.

"But I'd be happy to pitch in wherever I can. If your father's looking to tear down and remodel or whatnot." I squeeze my eyes closed. "I have some money in savings—"

"No."

"Jude is well off. Ever since he signed with the Indy Ice. He'd probably jump at the chance to help your family. I think his team does a lot of charity work already."

"Henry, I appreciate your concern. But I didn't come over here for a solution. I just wanted to make you aware of the situation."

I note the wariness in my friend's eyes. "I see."

"And I'd never ask you or Jude for money. And *Dat* would never accept it from someone outside the family. He wouldn't even want me talking to you about it."

"It doesn't have to be from me. I could give it to *you*."

He shakes his head. "Henry, I'm not taking your money. But I did want to point out the obvious."

I lower my brow. It mustn't be *that* obvious if I have no clue what he's talking about.

"Ellie," he says. Like I should understand his unsaid words. But I don't.

"Ellie?"

"You should probably keep your distance."

Oh, no. He wants me to stop seeing Ellie altogether? I respect my friend, but this is one thing I'm not sure I can comply with.

"My folks won't be able to afford a proper wedding anytime soon, I guess that is what I'm getting at."

Oh. *Oh.* "Does this mean—?"

"*Jah*, I think Ellie is finally coming around. But she won't have much time for courting or anything else. She's looking into taking a job in town." Eli frowns and shakes his head. "I hate not being able to provide for the womenfolk."

"It's no one's fault that you have siblings with medical needs, Eli. That would drain anyone's family resources."

His look is glum. "I still hate it."

"So, Ellie has taken a shining to me, has she?" I raise my eyebrows twice.

"Must've been the whoopie pies." Eli teases.

"Must have. If I would have known that, I would have made them a couple of years ago."

"Did you ever apologize to her?"

Again, I'm at a loss at Eli's meaning. "For...kissing her?"

"For stealing her lunch in fourth grade, *dummkopp.*"

"What?"

"That's the reason she's been peeved at you this

whole time." He swirls the remaining coffee around in his mug.

I frown. "You're kidding."

"It was a special lunch—a rare lunch."

"Oh. I had no idea." I shake my head. "Not that I should have been stealing lunches anyhow. There's no excuse for that. I was such a *dummkopp*."

"Well, there you have it. Mystery solved."

"I need to make an apology, then. For sure and for certain."

Eli nods. "I'd say that would be appropriate."

I know he warned me away but, I can't help but ask. "Do you think she'd join me for a picnic soon?" I grin. Because a picnic with Ellie sounds amazing.

Eli shakes his head, his lips curling up. "You're not about to keep your distance, are you?"

"Can you blame me after how long I've waited?"

Eli sighs. "I suppose not. You can ask her tonight when we come over to skate on the pond. Just promise me you'll keep things...above reproach."

"I'd never take advantage of your *schweschder*. I can promise you that." As far as kissing Ellie goes, well... can one keep a thirsty man from water?

Eli relinquishes a satisfactory nod.

And all of a sudden, I can't wait until tonight.

CHAPTER 15

ELLIE

"You ready to go?" Eli pops his head into my room. His ice hockey skates dangle from his arm, socks sticking out the top. "Duke's all hitched up."

"I'm not going tonight." I spare him a quick glance before I continue to survey the array of fabrics I laid out on my bed, trying to figure out how many items I'll be able to sew this evening. If I make simple items, I can get quite a few finished and prepared to sell. I always try to make my items look prettier by adding a fancy ribbon or even a piece of twine, along with a simple but cute handwritten tag. Special touches make me smile.

"What? Why not?"

In my mind, I'm thinking it's obvious. But I've learned over the years that sometimes brothers can be clueless and need things spelled out for them.

"I need to get my projects done before I go see Missy tomorrow. I want to take as many as possible." I frown. "I never knew Ivan Miller's place would be so motivating."

"Right?" Eli rolls his eyes. "What am I going to say to Henry? He wanted to talk to you."

I scoff. "And you were going to *let* him?"

"Maybe." I know he's teasing by the grin inching up one side of his mouth.

"I can't. I have too much work to do. I have to help out as much as I can, Eli. It would be selfish for me to go when I need to be here. Can you just tell Henry that I'll see him at the singing on Sunday?" I hate that I can't go and have fun with the others, but this is where I need to be.

Eli's eyebrows lift. "Does this mean you'll go riding with him?"

"Maybe." I say, throwing Eli's word back at him. Then I shrug, as though I haven't been thinking about Henry and our kisses every waking moment. "If he asks nicely."

Elijah snorts as though he's reading my mind.

"Whatever. Okay, I'll tell him. That should make him happy enough. You just better hope some other *maedel* doesn't turn his eye tonight."

I spin around and stare at my brother. "What?"

"You know Nancy Eicher has had her *kapp* set toward Henry for quite some time." Eli's trying to bait me and I know it.

"Many a *maedel* has their *kapp* set toward Henry Yoder. He's a handsome guy." I shrug, then point at my brother. "And don't you dare tell him I said that. He's prideful enough."

Elijah just shakes his head. "It's your loss. As for me, hockey helps to relieve some of my stress."

"You've been working all day. You deserve a break, *bruder*. Go have fun without me." I try to assure him.

"You deserve a break too, you know? I know you've been helping *Mamm* with the *kinner*." He sighs. "Are you sure you don't want to go?"

"This is where I need to be. And sewing helps relieve *my* stress."

Eli eventually gives up and walks down the hall. My heart pangs just a smidgen as I watch him go without me.

But I remain happy.

Happy that Elijah will be able to work out some of

his stress while doing something he loves with his friends.

Happy that I'll be able to pitch in for our family and contribute to the farm fund.

Happy that I might just allow Henry Yoder to court me.

CHAPTER 16

ENRY
As the area near the barn congests with horses and buggies, I eagerly await one specific carriage in particular—the one carrying the apple of my eye.

But Eli has been working at the factory all day, then he and Ellie will eat supper with the family, so I expect they'll be arriving a little later than everyone else. Since Eli and his father and others in the community who work at the factory hire an *Englischer* to take them back and forth to work every day, they're at the mercy of everyone else's schedule. Which meant that if some of the other Amish passengers in the van wanted to stop at the store or whatnot, arriving home could end up being pretty late. It's part of being Amish.

I know all about it firsthand, since the construction crew I work with also hires *Englischers* to drive us to jobs that are a little farther out, which are most of them. It's not so bad, but I find myself just wanting to get home at the end of a long workday.

I can only imagine how it must be for the married men on our work crew. If I was going home to Ellie every evening, I'd be tempted to hire my own driver just so I could get home sooner. Which might be an option for the future, Lord willing.

And here I am getting ahead of myself, because technically, Ellie and I haven't even been on a real date yet. But I'm hoping all of that will be changing soon, now that she actually acknowledges that I exist.

And tonight? Well, let's just say I've been bursting at the seams to lay my eyes on her. Whatever happens after that will be anyone's guess. Because with Ellie, I never know.

I hadn't expected to get to kiss her in Simon's buggy. I hadn't expected her to be inside my bedroom looking downright adorable in my cowboy hat. And for sure and certain, I didn't expect her to tackle me on my bed.

But if Ellie wants to shower me with affection, I'm not about to complain. As a matter of fact, I love her spontaneity. I love the thrill of not knowing what she's going to do next.

Which is why, when Elijah rolls up in his buggy alone, I'm taken off guard.

"Where's Ellie?" I blurt out, sticking my head inside his carriage.

"She wanted to stay home." Eli steps down and leads his horse to a stall. I follow him.

At Eli's words, my hope plummets. Because this news is devastating. She'd rather be *at home* than be around me?

At *home*? Really?

Jah, I'm selfish and a little pathetic. But after yesterday, I thought we'd crossed a bridge.

I thought we'd moved a mountain.

I thought we'd spotted the Promise Land off in the distance.

I thought...

I thought...

"Don't look so glum. She isn't ignoring you. She's taking some sewing projects into town tomorrow and wanted to finish as many as she could. You know, to help contribute to the farm fund and all."

And now it all makes sense. My insides warm as I think of Ellie's selfless giving spirit. Someday, I hope to be the recipient of it. But I need to be patient. A woman like Ellie will require some wooing.

"She did say to tell you that she would see you at the singing on Sunday." Eli adds.

"She did? Does that mean—?" Do I even dare hope?

"I'm thinking your chances are getting better all the time." Eli grins.

"Yee ha!" If I had been wearing my *verboten* cowboy hat, I would have thrown it in the air. I could kiss Eli. But I won't because he already mentioned the marriage thing after eating the whoopie pies and...now my thoughts are rambling. I'm sorry. I can't help it. Do you realize *how long* I've been waiting for this?

Eli just laughs, then walks toward the pond where the hockey game has been going on for the last half hour. We'll probably need to get out the glow-in-the-dark hockey pucks soon, since it's getting darker. They're great for when someone hits the puck into a snowbank. Nothing cooler than glowing snow.

But I can't even think about playing hockey right now. I'm shocked hockeyless. And maybe that wasn't a thing before, but it is now. Like the time Eli sent a puck flying into my face.

If all the *youngie* weren't congregated on my property, I'd go over to Ellie's right this instant. Not to annoy her or anything but just to say hello and bring her a snack or something. Maybe just sit and admire her as she works on her sewing projects. I'm dying to be near her. Yet, I can't.

But maybe tomorrow?

CHAPTER 17

ELLIE

After I thank the driver, she waits patiently while I snatch my tote bag filled with all the handmade items I managed to make since the last time I brought inventory to Trinkets and Treasures. I ask her to wait while I go inside and speak with Missy about possible employment opportunities.

"Hi, Ellie!" Her eyes light up when she spots my tote bag. "Ooh, let's see what you brought me today!" Missy rubs her hands together as she reaches into my tote bag and pulls out various items, oohing and aahing over each one.

"Missy, I was wondering something else." I suddenly felt nervous. I know most *Englischer* jobs require at the minimum a high school diploma. Since I only completed eighth grade in Amish school, I probably wasn't anybody's first choice for an employee. "Could I get a job here?"

Missy's eyes widen. "Oh. You'd want to work *here*? And that would be okay with your Amish church and all that?"

I nod. "We are permitted to work outside the home if needed. My brother works at the RV factory."

"Well, let me see. I'd have to train you. Unless you already know how to use one of these." She holds up an electronic device that is larger than a cell phone, but smaller than a computer. "My tablet."

I shake my head. "I've seen those, but I've never used one. But I can learn. I've used a smartphone before." Only once, to make a call to my *dat* when *Mamm* and I went to a doctor's appointment for the twins, little Andy and Alvin, and *Mamm* needed to ask *Dat* about purchasing new medications. But Missy didn't need to know that.

"Okay, it shouldn't be too difficult for you, then." She glanced around the shop. "I don't have a lot of extra work to keep us both busy full time, but I suppose I can use some extra help now and then. When would you be able to start?"

"I can start as soon as possible. If I begin right now, though, I will need to let my driver know." I glance out the window to be sure my driver is still waiting.

"Would starting tomorrow work for you? That way, I can figure out what I want you to do. We open up at nine, so if you could be here by ten, that would be great."

I feel my cheeks tighten as I smile. "Thank you so much." I turn to go.

"Oh, and Ellie? I think your new items are going to sell just fine." Missy's kind grin warms my insides.

I thank Missy again, then rush out of the store. I can't wait to tell Elijah the moment he returns home. I got a job!

After making a couple of other stops, the driver finally pulls into our driveway.

Since *Mamm* needed to use the family buggy today, I had to hire a ride. I would have asked Eli to use his courting buggy, but he tends to be particular about loaning it out. He treats it like a *boppli*, actually. "I want to keep it as nice as possible, because I never know if the *maedel* I'm taking home on Sunday might be my future *fraa*," he says. "Besides, we don't have money to fix it if something happens to it."

Part of me is surprised that *Dat* hasn't sold off Elijah's buggy yet. Who knows? At the rate things are going, it could be next.

Since it was colder out today, I didn't even ask. Besides, a warm enclosed car with the heater blowing is way more comfortable than having to pile on the quilts when the air is frigid.

The moment I step into the house, I know something is wrong.

"Isaac, where's *Mamm*?" I ask my fifteen-year-old brother, who is holding our youngest brother, Oscar. After Elijah, then me, Isaac is next in line. He's usually not in the house during the day, but out in the barn or in the field working with the animals. He's certainly not the one who is put in charge of the youngest siblings, but our thirteen-year-old sister Anna is nowhere in sight.

Isaac's eyes are wide. "It's Anna. *Mamm* and the *boppli* had to go with her in the ambulance."

Oh, no. Now there is something wrong with Anna too? My heartbeat quickens. This is the last thing our family needs. We can't afford to pay for a ride in an ambulance. *Dat* says it's better to hire a driver, but the situation must've been urgent.

"What happened? Tell me everything." I demand.

"I don't know exactly. I was outside in the barn when David came in to use the phone to call 911. Anna couldn't breathe, is what he told them. He said her lips were turning blue and she had red bumps all over." Poor Isaac looks terrified.

I take a squirming Oscar, our two-year-old brother, from Isaac's arms. "It sounds like she had an allergic reaction. Did she eat something with peanuts in it?"

"I don't know. Must be, though. *Mamm* thought she grew out of it."

I open the pantry, then hand Oscar a cookie to calm him down. "Did they say anything else? Did you see Anna before they left? Did she look better?"

"*Jah*, a little. They gave her a shot. But they insisted on taking her to the hospital."

"Poor Anna." No doubt, she'll probably need expensive medicines now too.

Mamm and *Dat* just can't seem to get a break. At church last week, the deacon said the community fund has been getting low. When he made the announcement, I could feel the eyes of the *g'may* move to our family. *Jah*, we'd required a lot when Emma needed her open-heart surgery, and *Mamm* and *Dat* still make regular payments to the hospital and would continue to for quite some time. But insurance is too expensive for my folks to afford, and the leaders forbid the use of government assistance. What else was my family to do?

"It's going to cost a lot of money, ain't so?" Isaac voices my thoughts.

"Do you think they'll have another dinner and auction soon?" Ten-year-old David joins in the conversation.

Isaac shrugs. "I don't know, but now that Ellie's here to watch the *kinner*, we best get back out to the barn and finish putting the hay up before *Dat* gets home."

David turns pitiful pleading eyes on me. "I was hoping Ellie would make us a snack first."

"What would you like?" I quiz.

"A sandwich?" He bounces on his toes.

I look at the loaf of bread and sigh. Since *Mamm* and *Anna* aren't home, it looks like I'll need to make more tomorrow morning. Which means I won't be able to work at Trinkets and Treasures.

"We're running low on bread, so you and Isaac can have a half sandwich each."

"Okay." I hear the disappointment in David's tone, and my heart hurts just a little. Our family has never starved, but we're used to going without.

Which was why the whole lunch thing with Henry was such a big deal to me.

"Why don't you each take half a banana too?" I know bananas aren't David's favorite, but if he's hungry he won't reject it.

"Okay." He reaches for a banana and gives Isaac half while I make up their sandwich.

"We need to eat quick, David. *Dat* and Eli might be coming home early if *Mamm* called him." Isaac barely chews his half of the banana before I hand each of them their half of the ham sandwich.

David peeks inside. "No cheese?"

I shrug. "Sorry, we're all out." Another item that will need to be added to our growing shopping list.

As the boys head outside, I bow my head and say a prayer for Anna and *Mamm* and *Dat* and the rest of our family. Somehow, with *Der Herr's* help, we will make it through yet another trial. But I can't help but wonder. When will the trials end? Will we ever find reprieve from these financial burdens?

CHAPTER 18

ENRY

Eli takes me aside before the church service this morning and informs me of the latest Petersheim woes. The moment I hear the news about Elijah's sister Anna, I shake my head. I vow then and there to donate extra money to the community fund and bid high come auction time.

I don't have millions of dollars, but I'm doing alright in construction. And my parents' place is all paid off so bills are low. I would just hand the money to Eli's *dat* if he'd accept it, but I know he wouldn't.

The verse about a man's pride bringing him low comes to mind, but if I were in his shoes, I'd likely feel the same way, so I don't judge. The only blessings I have are from *Der Herr* anyhow, so I have no right to think I'm any better. Just one wrong move and I could fall off a ladder or a roof and end up with a buggy load of bills of my own.

Still, my heart is heavy for my best friend's family. I can think of little else during the church meeting.

When the deacon makes the announcement about the auction to the *g'may*, my eyes immediately seek out Ellie, but she keeps her gaze on the *boppli* in her arms.

Ellie is perfect for me in so many ways. Just the fact that she and her family have had to overcome so much adversity tells me she is a strong woman. And being the eldest of the girls assures me that she is proficient in the kitchen and with child rearing. There isn't a single thing about her that I don't admire.

Okay, so she chucked my whoopie pies in the trash. That was something I wouldn't have imagined, especially since their financial situation is what it is. She must've been *really* mad at me to have done that. I can only imagine the tongue lashing she must've received at the time.

At least she tried them. But, as great as those whoopie pies were, I don't believe for a minute that she ate them all by herself. One thing I know about Ellie for a fact is that she is not selfish. I have no doubt she shared them with the entire family.

I'm dying to talk to Ellie but I have to wait until

the young folks' gathering tonight. But I need assurance from Eli that she will actually be in attendance, so I pull him aside.

"You and Ellie are still coming tonight, *ain't not*?"

"*Jah.*"

"Good. And you think she'll actually agree to ride with me this time?" I don't dare get my hopes up after my previous attempts at courting Ellie Petersheim. But considering our kisses, I'm more hopeful than ever. Nevertheless, doubt still nags.

Eli shrugs noncommittally. "I'll mention it to her. Although, she did say something about owing Simon a buggy ride."

"Simon?" I practically shout the name, drawing the attention of everyone around us.

Including Simon, apparently, who comes walking over. "Did someone call me?" Oh, good grief!

I groan. "*Nee.* I'm taking Ellie home tonight."

Simon chuckles. "*Right.* Well, good luck. Oh, and by the way, thank you for the hundred bucks. I think Ellie's really going to enjoy the new speakers I installed." He squeezes my shoulder. "I couldn't have done it without you."

His tone grates on me, and I can't stop my fists from balling. If I believed in fighting, I'd have it out with him right now. "What is *that* supposed to mean?" I grind out the words.

"You have competition. I asked her too." Simon smirks.

"Has she kissed you?" I have to ask. Panic seizes my chest and all kinds of things fly through my mind. They're probably irrational, but still. I don't think Ellie is the kind of woman to go around kissing every guy, but she did sort of attack me, so I'm questioning myself now. Maybe I'm not as special as I thought I was. *Ach*, this was turning into a nightmare.

Simon laughs again. "Wouldn't you like to know?"

Alright, that's it.

I'm about to get in Simon's face, when Eli steps between us and places a hand on my chest. He looks at me and shakes his head. Then he pulls me away from Simon and lowers his voice. "If you're looking to win my *schweschder*, this is not the way."

"Did. You. Hear. Him?" I am hot, as adrenaline pumps through my entire body. I thrust a thumb over my shoulder where Simon is now retreating.

"Simon's bluffing. He's just trying to rile you up. You need to ignore him." Eli's words hold merit. "Besides, fighting is the quickest way to change Ellie's mind."

"Change...but I thought you said..."

"I don't know for sure. But if I had to bet, I'd say the odds are in your favor."

"What's this I hear about betting?" The deacon comes near, scrutinizing me and Eli. "Have you two been frequenting that new casino?"

I'm horrified at the deacon's words. Not that I haven't been tempted to peek in and see what it's all about. Or pretend that I've never even heard about the casino and ask the deacon if *he's* been frequenting it. But even I'm not that *dumm*.

Instead, I say, "*Nee.*" My word is forceful, and it seems to mollify the deacon.

"Just a figure of speech." Eli gives a nonchalant shrug. "No casinos involved."

"We must be careful what we allow our mouths to utter. There are *kinner* who can be influenced by our words." The deacon's somber tone cuts to the quick. Leave it to the deacon to take us to task.

"We'll have to remember that." I say.

But now that the deacon mentioned it, I've got the casino on my mind. Now, *who* should be watching their words, huh?

Wow, I've gotten pretty good at the whole "holding my tongue" thing. Sometimes, I even impress myself.

"You'll do well to." The deacon nods then walks

off to a group of elders, probably to inform them of our irreverent speech.

As soon as Eli and I are alone, he bursts into laughter. "That was a close one, ain't not?"

"For some reason, I can't stop thinking about the casino now." I join in.

"Ellie will *not* want to go to the casino."

At the sound of her name, I'm back on track.

I send up a brief prayer. *Please,* Gott, *let Ellie agree to ride with me tonight.*

CHAPTER 19

ELLIE

My cheeks are on fire. I throw my hands up and cover my face, although I'm not sure my brother even sees me in his dark buggy.

"Come on, Ellie. I told Henry you'd probably say yes." Elijah goads as we inch closer to the Yutzys' where we'll be having the singing tonight.

I know I should be ready for this, but I'm not. I've rejected Henry's offer so many times, agreeing now just seems wrong.

"You've already kissed him, for crying out loud!" He shakes his head. "You women make no sense."

It makes perfect sense to me. It's not my fault my *bruder* is too *dumm* to understand. "But what about Simon?"

"You don't give a fig about Simon, Ellie!"

I cross my arms and sit up all proper-like. Not that Eli sees me this time, either. Where is the moon tonight, anyhow? "And how do you know?"

"Have you kissed him like you've kissed Henry?"

I gasp. Kiss Simon? Yuck. "Of course, not!"

"I rest my case," Eli says as we finally pull into the Yutzys' lane and drive toward the barn. "I'll tell Henry you said yes."

Eli jumps down from his side of the buggy, leaving me speechless. With dry heaves. Or night sweats. Okay, I'm not really sweating or vomiting, but my stomach *is* doing somersaults.

Because up until now, I've only been having fun. Casually riding with *bu*, knowing that nothing would come of it. That's why I was going to ride with Simon. He was safe. Boring, even. My heart was safe.

But tonight? With Henry? It feels *anything* but safe. Or boring.

My hands tremble as Henry makes his way toward me. I still can't believe this is happening.

His fingers rest on my dress sleeve, leaving a zing of

warmth on my skin. "Ready to go, Ellie?" Has his voice always rumbled low and tempting like that?

I. Am. In. *So*. Much. Trouble.

I nod and try to say yes, but it sounds more like a peep.

"I'll bring my buggy around." He grins. "Meet me by the back door?"

At the mention of his buggy, I finally find my bearings. "Your buggy? Not Simon's tonight?" I tease.

Henry laughs now. "That ol' thing? No way. Nothing but the best for you." He winks, then saunters off before I have a chance to reply.

My heartbeat quickens as I make my way toward the back door.

Eli stops me with a hand on my arm. My eyes meet my brother's. "What is it?"

"Ellie." He gives me a look. "Behave yourself."

"Me?" I squeak.

"Yes, *you*. No shotgun weddings, okay?"

We've watched enough old westerns in secret at Jude's house for me to understand what he means. But I gasp when I realize his implication, then give him a shove.

As I walk out the door, I hear his chuckle echoing behind me, and I shake my head.

As soon as I step outside, Henry's eye catches mine

and he hops down and offers his arm. I take it and we round the buggy. "What's that look all about?"

"*Ach*, just my *bruder* being a *dummkopp*." I would never reiterate Eli's words in front of Henry. I would die of embarrassment on the spot.

"I see."

Oh, but I'm glad he *can't* see in this instance.

"I have a surprise planned." He covers me with a lap robe, and I can see the gleam of his grin even in the dark. "Mind if we stop by my place before I take you home?"

Henry's house? Just the two of us? I gulp. "Is Ivy or your *mamm* there?" I hear the nervousness in my voice.

The buggy dips as he enters on the other side, and I'm super aware of his presence as his thigh slides next to mine. He smells really good tonight. "*Nee*, it'll just be us. But we won't be going inside the house. Unless you, um, need to."

"I don't," I blurt out.

"The surprise is in the barn." He nods, and I wonder if there is a new litter of kittens I haven't seen. I've always loved kittens.

"Okay." At the thought of kittens, I allow myself to relax awhile. But it proves difficult with our bodies so close.

"You warm enough?" Henry holds the reins steady as we travel toward the Yoders' property.

"*Jah.*" Am I warm enough? I want to laugh. Just being close to Henry makes me feel like I'm on fire. I wonder if his seat is this narrow on purpose as his arm —and everything else on his left side—is constantly brushing against me. I get the *ferhoodled* notion to wrap my hand around his bicep, but I force myself to ignore the urge.

Goodness, what is wrong with me? I remind myself that this is Henry Yoder. The boy I've loathed for almost a decade.

Henry is quiet and I wonder what he's thinking, but I refrain from asking.

"For the life of me, I can't think of anything to say." He chuckles.

"*Jah.* Me neither."

He reaches over and squeezes my hand. "I'm still having a hard time believing you finally said yes to riding with me."

"*Jah.* Me too."

His arm nudges mine. "You're very agreeable tonight."

I nod, confirming his words.

He chuckles. "Well, then, I hope you'll be agreeable to other things too."

"Other. *Things*?" My voice squeaks, and Elijah's words about a shotgun wedding pop into my mind.

"Like agreeing to court me." He studies me now, hope showing in his eyes.

"I thought that's what we were doing."

"I mean for real, Ellie. Not just tonight." His voice holds so much conviction I want to say yes on the spot. But I can't. This is Henry Yoder, after all.

"I'm...I..." and I'm at a loss for words.

"Can we just see how tonight goes? We can take it a day at a time, if you'd like." He inhales deeply. "But make no mistake about it, Ellie Petersheim. I aim to make you fall in love with me."

At his words, my gaze flies upward and tangles with his. For sure and certain I cannot fall in love with Henry Yoder.

Ever-so-gently, he takes my hand in his and brings it to his warm lips.

I gulp. I was right.

I. Am. In. *So*. Much. Trouble.

CHAPTER 20

ENRY

This is the happiest day of my life.

Honestly, I wasn't sure that Ellie Petersheim would *ever* agree to riding with me. But here we are.

I'm having a difficult time wearing any other expression than a gigantic smile. Seriously. I can't seem to wipe it off my face.

But I need to reel my emotions in. Because now that Ellie is finally sitting here next to me, I don't want to scare her off. I can already tell that she's as skittish as a newborn colt. I need to be smart and keep my wits about me.

I pull up to the hitching post by the barn and I notice my hands are trembling. *Get it together, Yoder.*

"Here we are." I train my voice, doing my best to sound nonchalant. But I'm anything but. This is the most momentous night of my life. And if I mess it up...

No, I'm not going to go there. I need to believe this is all going to go according to plan. *A man's heart deviseth his way: but the LORD directeth his steps.*

"Ach, I know, Lord." I mumble.

"What was that?" Ellie glances my way.

"Ach, just praying." I wave my hand in front of my face and shake my head. "Just ignore me. I'm feeling a little *ferhoodled,* if you must know."

"Jah, you and me both."

"Good. Then I guess we'll be *ferhoodled* together." I chuckle and she smiles.

I like smiles. Smiles are good.

I reach for her hand and help her down from the buggy, which puts her directly in front of me. A floral scent finds its way to my nostrils, and I realize she may have dabbed on a little perfume. For *me.*

That little fact has my mind flipping cartwheels. It shouldn't, but my heart begins an erratic beat. But I need to reel it in.

When our gazes meet, I come to my senses and step back. Because the last thing I want is to do something stupid like scare her off by kissing her right off the bat.

Jah, I am hoping for a *buss*, but I feel like I need to earn it first.

After securing Pistol, my mare, I reach for Ellie's hand. "*Kumm.*"

I point toward the barn opening. I've kept it mostly closed so it won't be too cold. I made sure to clean out all the stalls yesterday and lay fresh straw, so the stench isn't overbearing. But being raised on a farm, Ellie should be as used to this as I am. I was tempted to add air freshener, but that just seemed weird. Barns aren't supposed to smell like crisp linen sheets, or whatever the spray *mamm* uses is called.

As soon as we step inside, darkness engulfs us. Like second nature, I reach for my headlamp I keep on a wall peg just inside. I hand Ivy's headlamp to Ellie.

Immediately, we're bathed in light, and she smiles.

My heart is pinging all over the place. Ellie Petersheim has to be the prettiest girl ever. And she *chose* to ride with *me* tonight. *Denki, Gott.*

"It's in the loft." I point upwards and start climbing. "Follow me."

I would allow her to ascend the wooden ladder first, but she's wearing a dress, and somehow, me being behind her just feels wrong. At the same time, if she were to slip and fall, I'd feel guilty for not being there to catch her. It's a lose-lose situation, really.

Now, if we were married, I'd relish the chance to walk up behind her. Then her wearing a dress and her hips swaying and driving me wild in the process wouldn't be an issue. *Ach*. I shake my head to clear my thoughts.

"*Ach*, what is this?" The pleasure in her tone, although hesitant, warms me from the inside out.

I beckon her to follow me inside the cozy enclosure. I worked all afternoon moving hay bales to create a little cove around the quilt I laid for our picnic. In the middle of the quilt sat *Mamm's* largest roasting pan.

"Sit." I invite her to sit on one of the pillows I snagged from my bed.

She does and I sit across from her with the closed roasting pan between us. "Are you warm enough? I brought the lap robe up."

I hand it to her, and she places it over her lap. "That's better."

"Okay, before I open this, I need to explain. I talked to your brother the other day and he mentioned something to me." I take her hands in mine and meet her cautious, beautiful eyes. I take a deep breath, suddenly feeling nervous. "Ellie Petersheim, I was a real jerk back in fourth grade when I stole your lunch. It was wrong in so many ways. And you don't know how many times I've kicked myself since discovering why you've hated me all these years. I wish I had known sooner so I could have apologized. But I didn't. So, I'm apologizing right now."

I try to read her expression, but her thoughts are hidden from me. I press on. "Will you please, please forgive me for being such a *dummkopp*?"

I hold my breath in anticipation.

CHAPTER 21

*E*LLIE

I stare into Henry's earnest eyes while he waits for my reply.

I've waited so long for this apology, and yet, I feel like I've already forgiven him. "*Jah*, Henry. I can forgive you."

He sighs in relief. "*Denki.*"

Then a thought occurs to me. I was unfair to him by punishing him all this time when he really had no idea why. *Jah*, it was wrong of him to take my lunch. There's no denying that. But I could have handled it better. "If you'll forgive me too for holding a grudge so long."

"There's absolutely nothing to forgive. I was a jerk,

and I deserved to be loathed. No fourth grader should ever have to go hungry at lunch. I still can't believe I was that mean back then." He shakes his head, berating himself.

"That wasn't a yes." I say.

"*Nee*, it wasn't. But if you feel like you need to be granted forgiveness, it's yours. Now and always."

"Always?"

"*Jah*." He rubs his handsome jaw that has tiny whiskers poking through. "I do wonder about something, though."

I tilt my head in question.

"Why didn't you tell the teacher on me? Or your brother?"

"My brother, because I didn't want to be accused of being a tattletale. And I didn't tell the teacher because we had a mean substitute teacher, and I didn't want to be the reason you got paddled."

"Really?" He quirks a smile. "So, you *did* like me at least a *little* bit back then?"

"Full confession. Up until that incident, I may have had a teensy-weensy crush on you." I slap my hand over my mouth. I can't believe I just admitted that to Henry Yoder.

"No kidding? Ellie Petersheim was crushing on

me?" He twists a wry smile. "I don't know if I can believe that."

I shrug.

"Wow. Ellie Petersheim actually *liked* me at one point in time. This really is the best day of my life. Especially now that you've forgiven me. Which reminds me." He clears his throat and points his finger in the air. "Ellie Petersheim, I, Henry Yoder, do hereby present you with…your lunch!" He pulls the lid off the roasting pan that is filled with heart-shaped sandwiches, bags of barbeque potato chips, apples, and whoopie pies.

I laugh, but my eyes widen at the abundance. "Why so much?"

"Well, remember the story in the Bible about Zacchaeus? When he discovered that he was wicked and he'd cheated people, he vowed to pay them back fourfold. So, there are four sandwiches, four apples, four bags of chips, and four whoopie pies. All for you." His grin widens.

I laugh again. "I can't possibly eat that much. And I thought I counted six?"

"I put two of each in there for me too." He shrugs.

"I would have shared. It isn't like I can eat all this." The gesture is really sweet, though. I lean over and peck him on the cheek. "*Denki*, Henry. This is so sweet. And unnecessary. But sweet just the same."

At that moment, his stomach rumbles and we both chuckle.

"Maybe we should pray, *jah*?" He bows his head, and I follow suit.

CHAPTER 22

ENRY

This evening is going even better than I imagined.

Hearing that Ellie used to have a crush on me —*me*—has me floored. Why did I have to go and ruin it? We could have been courting already. We could have been married at sixteen. Okay, maybe not that young. But most definitely by now.

I shake my head. "I still can't believe it. The prettiest girl alive had a crush on *me*."

Ellie snorts. "If you're trying to charm me, it's working."

"No charms. I'm just speaking the truth." I polish off my first sandwich, then dig into a bag of chips.

"I'm afraid I'm not all that hungry. May I get a take home box, sir?"

I laugh. "Sure. We'll have to go to the house, though."

A chilly breeze wafts through the barn and I shiver. "Wow. There's a bite in the air tonight."

She holds up the lap quilt. "Do you...? We can share."

I wasn't fishing for an invitation to be close to Ellie, but since she suggested, I'm not about to decline her offer. "*Denki.*"

I move around *Mamm's* roasting pan and plop down next to her on the quilt. When she lifts the blanket, I slide close to her and am immediately enveloped in warmth. "This is nice."

"*Jah.*"

She turns her head, and I realize how close we are. Being this close to Ellie spikes my pulse like nothing else, and I can think of little else besides kissing her. Truly, I hadn't planned on giving her a kiss until I dropped her off at home at the end of our evening.

I was going to exercise patience. Longsuffering.

When our eyes meet, she tugs her bottom lip between her teeth, and I can't help but be drawn to her mouth. Well, there goes the patience and longsuffering. I had good intentions.

But before I kiss her, I need to make sure I'm not misinterpreting the desire in her eyes.

I inch back and catch what I think might be disappointment on her face. "To avoid your brother clobbering me with his hockey stick or harnessing me with a rope and dragging me behind his buggy, I figured it might be safer to ask first, although I feel like I'm kind of killing the mo—"

"Henry Yoder, would you please stop talking and just kiss me?" Her eyes are sparkling with amusement.

"Yes, m—" And her lips are on mine.

I'm not sure what it is about kissing Ellie Petersheim, but my senses seem to take leave, and I could swear I'm transported to some type of fantasy world. Because having Ellie's lips on mine pretty much fulfills every fantasy I've ever had. Her kisses are perfection at its best.

Not that I'd actually swear. Okay, I *might* but I probably shouldn't admit it.

Ellie makes the faintest feminine sound and it drives me wild. One of my hands is cradling the back of her head and the other one is resting on her warm neck, and the only thing I can think of at the moment is how beautiful she must look with her hair down. I've only ever gotten a glimpse of her hair, confined by her prayer *kapp*.

Without even asking, I feel for the pins holding her *kapp* and remove them. Ellie doesn't protest, and I take her silence as permission to continue. I place her covering to the side, then pull out the hair pins holding her bun in place. When her hair tumbles over her shoulders and down her back, I can't help but slide my fingers through her silky unbound tresses.

My lips leave hers, trailing a warm path to her neck, where I bury my nose in her irresistibly soft hair. With the fire running through my veins, I no longer require the lap robe. We lean back, causing one of the bales of hay to plummet to the ground.

"Hey! You trying to kill me?" A familiar male voice from below the loft sounds.

Ellie squeaks as she pries her lips off mine and begins frantically gathering her hair. She leans down to hide, and as soon as I gather my wits about me I stand up to see my neighbor Jude with the bale of hay at his feet. *Jah*, that could have been bad. I'm glad he appears to be in one piece, and I didn't take him out for the season. Or ruin his hockey career altogether.

"I'm sorry, we were just...I mean *I* was just..." I must resemble a tomato. It's a good thing the barn is mostly dark.

"Moving hay in the dark?" There's amusement in

Jude's tone, but the knowing look in his eyes makes me squirm.

"What are you doing here anyway?"

"Hey, I tried the house, but no one answered. Sorry to interrupt you and Ellie." He winks. "But I wanted to stop by before I head out tonight. I've got a home game next Thursday, and I'm wondering if you and Ivy and Eli and Ellie would like to come. I brought you tickets." He holds up what is probably the aforementioned tickets, but I can't see them in the dark.

"Uh, *jah*. That would be great. I'll see if we all can go."

"Okay, then. And, if Ivy would like a jersey, I can get her one." Jude offers.

I want to growl. Ivy doesn't need to be wearing Jude's jersey. She's Amish, and as far as I know, she plans to stay that way. "*Nee*, she doesn't need one. She'll wear her Amish dress."

"Okay, then. I'll just leave the tickets right here on the saddle." Jude's footfalls sound as though he's leaving the barn, but then his voice echoes. "You two have fun. And stay out of trouble." I hear his laugh as he finally exits the barn.

"*Ach du liebe.*" I turn back to Ellie, who has now managed to gather her hair back into a bun and is pinning her *kapp* back into place. I reach over and remove a piece of straw from her hair, my smile apologetic.

"Should we box up the rest of the food?" Ellie asks. How she manages to stay calm, I'm unsure.

I sigh, realizing our previous fire has been doused. But maybe that's a good thing? "*Jah*. Let's go."

Thanks for ruining the moment, Jude.

CHAPTER 23

E*LLIE*

Aside from the embarrassing moment when his *Englisch* neighbor showed up, I'd say my date with Henry went well. He apologized several times, which wasn't necessary but thoughtful, nonetheless. It wasn't his fault our romantic moment got interrupted, after all.

When he went into the house to get something to take all my leftover food home in, I took the opportunity to use his restroom and check Ivy's hand mirror to see that my *kapp* was pinned on correctly and be sure I didn't have any more straw in my hair. Because I can only imagine the interrogation I'd receive from Elijah if he found even a speck of hay.

And then, what would I say? That I was rolling in the

hay with Henry in his haymow? It's not like I'm going to lie. If I tell the truth, though, my *bruder* very well might string Henry up to his buggy. Okay, maybe he wouldn't do something *that* extreme. We are nonresistant, after all. But I wouldn't want to find out what he'd do. Probably forbid me from seeing Henry Yoder again, at the least.

I am excited about going to a hockey game, though. Henry insisted he'd pay for all the extra stuff, i.e, the driver, hotel, and whatever else we required for the trip to Indy. I don't even know much about hockey other than what I've seen of the guys playing on the pond.

Henry said Jude's team is relatively new, but their team, Indy Ice, is up and coming. They show Jude on TV and everything. Henry warned me about that. The fact that we might possibly be on TV too has me nervous. I hope the deacon or bishop doesn't get a glimpse when they're eating out at one of those restaurants that have screens all over the place.

Also, since we're Amish, that will give people something extra to talk about, so there's a good chance we will be videoed.

Early the next morning, *Mamm* grins when I walk into the kitchen. "What is all this then?"

She holds out all the sandwiches and apples and

chips and whoopie pies. "More whoopie pies? Am I to believe they're from Henry?" Her countenance is hopeful.

I bite my lip, then feel my cheeks heat. "*Jah*. He made me a picnic last night."

"*Ach*, what a sweet boy." I'm afraid *Mamm* will only ever see Henry as a boy. She was likely around when Henry was a *boppli*, since both of our families have lived in the community for generations. "Am I to assume you and Henry are courting?"

"*Mamm*." I try my best *please don't ask* tone.

Elijah walks into the kitchen. "Yep, they're courting alright. At least, Ellie left the singing in Henry's buggy. And he dropped her off last night. It was pretty late too."

I use all my resolve not to swat my brother with a dishtowel. But I'm hoping he didn't see our goodnight kiss, because...*jah*.

"You're not getting any of my leftovers." I stick my tongue out at Eli, to *Mamm's* disapproval.

"Well, I'm glad you finally said yes to that boy. Henry's been pining over you for as long as I can remember, and all you've done is turn your nose up at him." *Mamm* has never mentioned that she noticed this, and it takes me by surprise.

I gasp and try to defend myself. "I had good reason. He was mean to me."

Mamm points to the food. "Then what do you call all this?"

"That's Henry making up for being mean." I swat Elijah's hand when he reaches for a whoopie pie.

Mamm frowns. "And you know you're not supposed to harbor unforgiveness in your heart."

"I've forgiven him now."

Mamm turns around at a knock on the backdoor. "Now who could that be at this hour?"

Eli goes to open the door, then returns with our visitor. "Look who I found." My brother smirks.

My eyes widen. "Henry? What are you doing here?"

"May I have a word with you, Ellie?" Henry's words and sheepish tone cause *Mamm* to practically swoon. *Oh, brother.*

I lead the way to the living area, where we can have a bit of privacy.

"I...uh...my work was called off today. So, I was thinking that maybe I can help you." His feet shuffle, like he might be second-guessing himself for coming over at this hour.

"Help me?"

"You know, with your sewing projects and what-not." He shrugs.

"Oh." I'm kind of at a loss for words. "Do you know how to sew?"

"*Ach, nee.* But maybe you can teach me?" Goodness, he's adorable. I love the vulnerability in his voice and his willingness to help.

"Aww...Henry wants to learn to sew." Elijah sings from the doorway.

"Elijah! *Geh*, now!" I love my brother, but he's on my last nerve this morning. "Isn't your driver here yet?" I tap my foot.

Dat shows up behind Elijah and cups his shoulder. "Hello, Henry. We'll be going now." *Dat* hauls a grinning Eli out the door.

Mamm appears in the doorway. "Henry, have you had any breakfast yet? I can pour you a cup of coffee and you and Ellie can sit at the table."

Henry nods. "*Denki*, I'd love some coffee. I brought you some eggs from our hens and bread that Ivy made. They're just in my buggy. I'll go get them."

And there goes my theory about his white teeth and not drinking coffee. Maybe I'll have to inquire about his toothpaste.

"Well, aren't you thoughtful?"

Henry smiles at me, then disappears out the door he entered through.

Mamm spins toward me. "Ellie, I'm telling you. That boy is a keeper. You better snatch him up before someone else does."

And at that moment I realize that *Mamm* is probably right.

By the end of the afternoon, Henry and I have sewn dozens of new items to take to Trinkets and Treasures. And I can't stop thinking about my very own newfound treasure.

Henry Yoder.

CHAPTER 24

ENRY

I've never seen the inside of the little shop where Ellie works, so I'm hoping to surprise her today with a visit.

I have no clue what her work hours are today, but my idea is to whisk her off on her break for a quick bite to eat. If I thought I was interested in Ellie before, now that I've gotten to know her even better, I can't seem to get enough of her. I want to be near her every waking moment—*ach*, and every sleeping moment, if I'm honest.

But, *Gott* willing, that will come in time.

I can't wait to see the look on her face when I walk through the door and she notices me there.

I pull the buggy around the back and park at the small lot near the alleyway. After checking my teeth in my rearview mirror, I hop down and make my way toward the entrance. I don't see the Petersheims' buggy anywhere, so Ellie must've hired a driver today. I hate that she has to use her hard-earned wages to pay for a driver. I wish I could take all the burdens from her slender shoulders, but that's not possible—yet.

Someday, I'd like to become her provider and take care of all her needs. But with the Petersheims' financial situation, it looks like someday might be a long, long way off. If only they'd let me help. I would have no problem whatsoever providing the funds needed for Ellie and me to get married.

And if Ellie and I did get married, wouldn't that ease the family's burden just a bit? It would be one less mouth to feed, not that Ellie eats all that much. On the other hand, it would be one less set of hands to help out at home.

Truly, I'm at a loss of what to do. Because the truth is, I'd marry Ellie tomorrow if I could. I don't want to wait years and years to make her my *fraa*. And at the rate we're going in the passion department, I don't think we *can* wait that long. Because Ellie's kisses...let's just say they light a fire in me.

Gott, *if there's anyway You could speed things along.*

Ach, jah, not the most reverent prayer I've ever uttered. *Sorry,* Gott. *Just please help me to have the patience I need to wait for Your perfect timing. But if it could be sooner rather than later, I would really, really appreciate it.* I'm not sure if the second prayer was any better, but I have a feeling *Der Herr* understands.

I walk inside and spot a few customers. My eyes scan the area where the cash register is, but Ellie is not behind the counter. Instead, a kind looking middle-aged woman is helping out a customer with their purchases. I don't want to disturb her, so I roam the shop in search of the woman I've fallen in love with.

My hope plummets when I discover she is nowhere to be found. As soon as the woman at the counter has a break in customers, I approach her. "Is Ellie around?"

Her eyes scan my attire and a soft smile appears. At that moment, I wonder if Ellie has mentioned anything about me—about us.

"I'm sorry, Ellie won't be in for a few more hours." At what must be my look of disappointment, she adds. "Is there something I can help you with?"

I think about her question for just a moment, then nod. "*Jah,* please. Where are the items she has for sale?"

Her grin widens and she rounds the counter. "Let me show you."

Even though I had already roamed the store, my mind had been solely focused on one thing—finding Ellie. But now that I'm actually looking for merchandise, I spot various items here and there, including some of the crafts I helped Ellie sew and package.

And if I do say so myself, they look quite appealing.

"My name is Missy. I'm the owner." The lady offers her hand to shake. "Are you a friend of Ellie's?"

"Yes. I'm her boyfriend."

Missy's eyes crinkle at the corners. "I thought you might be."

I see the various items Ellie has made in different sections of the store as Missy points them out. And then I'm struck with an idea. What if *I* purchase Ellie's handmade goods? I could give them as gifts. Or...better yet, I can donate them to the upcoming auction and she could maybe even get twice the money. No one would have to know that I was the one who purchased them.

"I have a question. I'd like to buy Ellie's merchandise, but I don't want her to know that it was me. So, if I buy several items, would you not tell her who purchased them?" I frown. "I know it must sound strange but—"

Missy pats my hand then winks. "Your secret's safe

with me. If she asks, I can just say a customer stopped in and purchased them. That's all she needs to know."

"I appreciate that. Could you bag up the items she's made for me?"

"Didn't you help her make some of the handi-crafts? I remember her saying that her beau came over and helped her sew." A knowing smile lights her face.

My cheeks warm. Not the manliest thing to admit. I nod sheepishly.

"That was just one of the sweetest things I'd ever heard. Most men would have passed that off as women's work. But in my opinion, there's nothing more manly than a man helping out his woman in whatever capacity she needs, whether it be doing the dishes, changing a diaper, or helping her sew. So, kudos to you for stepping up and being a real man. It's a rare trait, believe me."

"I'd do anything for Ellie." It was the truth, pure and simple.

"You're a true keeper. And I think I mentioned that to Ellie when she told me about you helping her. If you're trying to win her heart, keep it up. I do believe it is working, young man." Missy held up a stack of sewn goods. "And this, what you're doing here? It's priceless."

"Has Ellie mentioned anything to you about her family?"

Missy frowns. "The medical bills and such? Yes. She hasn't gone into a lot of detail, but I put two and two together when she came in and asked for a job."

"I was thinking of donating these to the auction our community is having to benefit the Petersheims. That way, she can get twice the money for them."

"Oh, you are such a dear." Missy shook her head. "You've inspired me. You know, Ellie has these here on consignment. Well, I think I will donate an extra portion for the cause as well."

"Thank you. I'm sure it will be appreciated."

Why was it that when you did a good deed for someone else, it brought immense pleasure to yourself? It's almost like *I'm* getting more of a blessing than the Petersheims. I can't help but feel like a million bucks as I drive home with several bags of Ellie's handmade goods. I wish I could see the look on her face when Missy tells her about the items that sold. The owner suggested that I not buy everything, so that Ellie wouldn't be overwhelmed trying to restock.

As it was, the items I purchased almost amounted to a couple thousand dollars. It was a hefty price tag, but I consider it an investment in my and Ellie's future. I may not be able to give money directly to the family, but this is a way I can help contribute to the cause without squelching Daniel Petersheim's pride.

Besides, it was between me and God. Nobody ever needed to know about the good deed done today.

Denki, Gott, for allowing me to help in this small way. Please bless Ellie and her family. Amen.

CHAPTER 25

LLIE
    I was supposed to be at work this morning, but *Mamm* needed me at home to help with the *kinner*. I really wanted to work for Missy so I could earn more money for the family, but I don't know how it's going to work out with my employment at Trinkets and Treasures.

I hate that I haven't proven to be a reliable employee, but I'm glad that Missy is understanding. I could never see a place like the RV factory where Elijah and *Dat* work being so accommodating. Working for Missy is a blessing, for sure and certain.

"Really, it's not a problem," Missy says as I walk through the door, apologizing once again. "I understand that your life is complicated right now. Just know that I'm here if you need someone to talk to."

"Thank you." I take off my traveling bonnet and head toward the employees' back room, to deposit my personal belongings.

When I return to the main store area, Missy says, "I do appreciate you giving me a call to let me know when you won't be able to make it."

"*Ach*, that's the least I can do. I don't know how I can contribute much to our family if I can't work." The thought is a little depressing.

"Well, I think your luck is changing." Missy's grin tells me she knows something I don't.

"What do you mean?" I begin looking around the store. "Wait. Did you move things around? I don't see the aprons I brought in. Or...what happened to the display of potholders?"

When I turn I see Missy's smile grow even wider. "They sold."

I look where the displays used to be. "All of them?"

She shakes her head vigorously. "Look around. That's not all."

I slowly walk around the shop, doing my best to recall the places we had my items on display. There are still a few but...*ach*, this was crazy! "Did...it looks like almost everything is gone."

Missy walks up to me and hands me what looks like a slip of paper. But when I look down, I realize it's a check.

"Two thousand thirty-five dollars?" Tears immediately pool in my eyes. *Mamm* and *Dat* will be so happy. "Missy, who bought this much stuff?"

"A customer." She shrugs.

"*Ach*, it must've been an angel!"

"You never know." Missy smiles. "But it looks like you might have quite a bit of work to do to restock our inventory."

I'm so excited, I clap my hands. "Do I ever! I've never sold this much. This is...it's crazy. Thank you so much!"

"No need to thank me."

"*Jah*, I couldn't have sold this much if you didn't let me keep my things here on display." Missy really is a Godsend.

"Your crafts draw people into the store, so it's a mutually beneficial setup. I'm glad to be able to sell them. People want to purchase authentic handmade Amish goods. And I think we sell your items at a reasonable enough price that folks who own bigger shops in tourist places can buy and resell them."

I'd never considered that. "Do you think that's what's happening?"

"You never know." Missy hands me a pen and notebook, then points to the empty display. "You'll need to jot down what you've sold so you can bring in new inventory."

"It's going to take a while for me to restock all that's sold." I still can't believe it.

"Well, maybe you can get that boyfriend of yours to help you again. Did you say his name was Henry?"

My heart warms at the mention of Henry's name. "*Ach, jah*. I can't wait to tell Henry that we sold his potholders. And everything else. He's going to be so excited!"

"It looks like you two might be spending a lot of time together. A man like that is rare, indeed. You might want to hold onto him." The twinkle in Missy's eye doesn't escape my notice.

Jah. I definitely want to hold onto Henry. In more ways than one.

CHAPTER 26

ENRY

Ellie beams at me the moment she steps into my house. "Your potholders sold, Henry!" I love that she's so excited. It sure beats the looks of disdain I used to receive. I'm just happy that she's finally mine.

I grin. "So, it was a good day?"

"The best ever! Some *Englischer* came in and bought up almost all my stuff. Can you believe that?"

An *Englischer*? Was that what Missy told her or is she just assuming?

"That's amazing," I say. But all I can think of at the moment is that I better get all that merchandise boxed up and sent to the auctioneer. Because if Ellie were to discover it in my room, I'd be in deep trouble. She'd probably be livid and hand the money right back to me.

"I'm going to be so busy trying to replace everything he bought."

My eyebrow arches. "He?"

She shrugs. "Or she. I didn't ask Missy."

"I see."

"So, um, I was thinking…" Her lips twist like she's trying to phrase the question I already know she's planning to ask.

"Would you like my help?" I offer.

"*Ach*, I think that would be *wunderbaar*."

"If you want, I could take my *mamm's* sewing machine to your place or I could bring yours here. Whichever you think would be best."

"For real? You'd do that?"

"*Ach*." I step close and brush my fingers against her hair. Then I lean down and brush her lips with mine. "Ellie Petersheim, don't you know I would do anything for you?"

"Henry." At my name, tears spring to the surface of her eyes. "Why are you being so nice to me?"

I can't take my eyes off her. This woman is everything to me. "I thought that was plain to see. I love you."

Her watery eyes search mine. "You do?"

I put my hand on my chest. "With all my heart."

I draw her into my embrace and kiss the top of her prayer *kapp*. I'd love to be able to ask for her hand in marriage, but I feel it's too soon. The last thing I want to do is scare her off by being overeager. So instead, I just hold her for several moments.

"You're too good to me. You know that?" She sniffles against my chest.

"I could never be too good. There's so much I want to give you, Ellie. So much I'd love to do for you." If only I could remove her burdens.

"I don't deserve your kindness."

I lift her chin and stare into her eyes. "Don't ever say that. Ellie Petersheim, you deserve the best of everything. Always."

Then I dip my head and claim the kiss I've been craving all day.

Jah, I need to have a chat with Daniel Petersheim, and soon. Because making Ellie my wife is nearly all I can think of.

CHAPTER 27

E*LLIE*

I can hardly believe auction day is already here. So many people have come out to attend the auction and breakfast. We are truly blessed to have all these folks who love and care for us, both Amish and *Englisch*.

Mamm and *Dat* were just as stunned as I was when I brought home the check from Trinkets and Treasures. They were grateful to be able to pay more toward the hospital bill. But all in all, it barely made a dent in the astronomical balance.

Henry and I have been busy sewing, and we delivered our next batch of handicrafts to Missy at Trinkets and Treasures. For sure and certain, I never imagined Henry and me sewing side by side, but there we were.

Elijah laughed every time he passed by, but Henry was a good sport.

True to his word, Henry really does seem like he'll do anything for me. A girl can't help but fall in love with a guy like that. Which has me thinking about a future with me and Henry in it. My thoughts have become so *ferhoodled* I've even tried to imagine what our *bopplin* will look like.

I don't know what has gotten into me. It's like I'm inside out and upside down a thousand times over.

"Hey, Ellie, look! Isn't that one of the aprons you made?" *Mamm* pointed out the next item up for auction.

"*Ach, jah.* That's one of the aprons I sold at Trinkets and Treasures. Whatever is it doing here?"

The auctioneer starts out at a really low price, then I hear a familiar voice holler, "Twenty dollars!"

When I pivot, sure enough, Henry is standing tall holding up his number. *Ach*, he must've known it was mine. I smile and shake my head.

"See?" *Mamm* sighs. "Henry is the one. Probably bid on that for you."

My cheeks warm, when Henry turns and grins at me.

Our gazes catch and I'm in a trance until I realize the next item up for auction is one of my aprons too.

Again, Henry bids twenty dollars, then is outbid. He bids again, then another person bids and wins.

"That one sold for thirty-five dollars!" I can hardly believe it. Although Henry didn't win the bid, he made the final price go up. Had that been his intention? The rascal. Although, I'm sure and certain Henry would have paid thirty dollars.

"I do believe you have captured that boy's heart." *Mamm* pats my hand.

After that, many more of my handsewn items come up for auction. It seems like the person who purchased them at Trinkets and Treasures just donated them all to be auctioned off. I shake my head in amazement. God is so good.

Surely, this auction and the breakfast have raised a great deal of money. Hopefully, it will be enough so *Mamm* and *Dat* won't have to sell the farm.

CHAPTER 28

H*ENRY*

I think this is the most nervous I've ever been.

I don't want Ellie to know I'm here, because I'd like to surprise her, so I wait until her father comes to the barn to tend to the chores. Before I ask Ellie to marry me, I want to be sure it is okay with her folks first.

Maybe I'm crazy to be here since Eli said his *dat* wouldn't let me pay for the wedding, but I need to at least try. If we want a date in the spring wedding lineup, I'm going to need to approach the leaders soon. Not to mention, Ellie and I will need to go through our baptism classes first.

"Daniel," I call out as he approaches the barn. I

note that Elijah and his brothers are headed out for chores as well. "Can we talk in private?"

"*Guten morgen*, Henry! What has you here on this fine day?" Daniel rarely seems to be without a smile, no matter how dire his circumstances. It's like he harbors some kind of secret joy. "*Kumm*, we can talk in my shop."

After he leads me to the back room in the barn, I unload my thoughts. But I need to tread carefully because Eli shared their family's circumstance with me in confidence. I have to act like I only know as much as the rest of the *g'may* knows, just that they have bills that have threatened to drown them. I can't let on about them possibly losing the house or, *Gott* forbid, their moving to the Millers' old shack.

"You know that I've been courting Ellie." I can't stop my smile. There was a time when I wasn't sure that would ever happen. Yet, here I am about to ask her father for permission to marry her. I still can't believe my good fortune.

"I've heard the rumors." His eyes sparkle.

"Well, I'm just going to say it. I want to marry Ellie this spring."

And his smile turns upside down. "So soon?"

"I know it seems sudden, but you must know that I've loved Ellie for years. And I think she might agree to it. I hope she will. If she doesn't, then I can wait until fall if I have to."

"I'm afraid that's not going to be possible. In spring or fall. Weddings, as you know, are no small matter."

"I realize that, and that's why I'd like to help pay—"

Daniel holds up a hand to stop my jabbering. "*Nee. I* will pay for my own *dochder's* wedding. When it is time. But now is not the time. Perhaps a couple of years down the road."

Ach, a couple of years? Right now, that seems like forever. And that's not even a guarantee.

How can I convey my thoughts without them sounding wrong? "I'm just worried that...well, I don't want to, um...do anything we shouldn't yet. You know what I mean?"

"Well, then, if you cannot contain, perhaps you and Ellie should take a step back. She's only eighteen yet. You will have plenty of time."

Jah, but I want to marry her yesterday. I don't want to wait for years on end. Nevertheless, this is Ellie's father, and I need to respect his wishes.

I rub my chin, but I can't squelch my disappointment. "*Ach, vell, denki* for hearing me out, anyhow."

Daniel grips my shoulder. "There's no one that me

or Ellie's *mamm* would rather see her marry more than you, Henry. It's a *gut* match. A wedding is just not going to be possible for some time. I'm sorry."

Well, that's that. I honestly don't know how we're going to be able to wait that long. Maybe it's best that I don't go say hi to Ellie this morning.

I've got a full work week ahead of me anyhow. I need to buckle down and attempt to refocus my thoughts.

Because, barring a miracle, making Ellie my *fraa* will be years in the making.

I'm going to need Your help, Lord!

CHAPTER 29

LLIE

I can't put my finger on what it is, but Henry seems off tonight. And although he has assured me everything is fine, I'm not convinced that is the case.

He's been unusually quiet since we began our buggy ride and he's sitting farther away than usual. Like he's trying not to touch me. I'm a little worried about him. About *us*.

"How are your sewing projects coming along?" He asks casually, as though he's not trying to take the focus off himself. There's something wrong, for sure and certain, that he doesn't want me to know about.

I sigh. "Fine."

"I'm sorry the auction and breakfast didn't bring

in as much as your *dat* had hoped." I can sense there's something else behind his words.

I shrug. "It was still a blessing. We can't make money appear out of thin air."

"*Nee*, I suppose not." He turns toward my house.

"Is your *mamm* or Ivy home tonight?" I'm a little surprised he isn't taking me by his house first.

He shrugs. "Ivy could be."

"What would you like to do tonight? We could play a game, and I can make some snacks."

He rubs the back of his neck like he's uncomfortable. "I, um, I'm a little tired tonight. I probably won't come in."

And that's when I *know* he's putting me off. I stare at him. "Henry, what's wrong?" I hear the small quiver in my voice, but I'm doing my best to keep my emotions in check.

"Nothing." He doesn't look at me but works his jaw. "I just have a full week ahead of me. I should probably get some rest."

He's making excuses and I know it. Because he's never chosen sleep or work over me. Has he changed his mind about us? My resolve begins to crumble at the thought.

When we pull up to the house, he doesn't move to get down but leans over and pecks me on the cheek.

"Good night, Ellie." Then he just sits there like he's waiting for me to leave.

Tears prick my eyes now. I don't want a peck on the cheek!

Henry's going to get a real kiss from me whether he wants one or not.

I take hold of his face and press my lips to his, but the kiss is just not the same. Henry doesn't move his lips or his head or anything. He's stiff and rigid.

I push back. "Fine! If that's what you want then I'm going inside."

I'm upset because Henry has never rejected me before, and now I just feel like a fool. What happened to the words he uttered just a few days ago about doing *anything* for me? About being *in love* with me? Well, there's none of that now. As a matter of fact, it feels like Henry doesn't even want to be near me.

Have I done something to make him not love me anymore?

I scramble down from the buggy and hurry toward the house.

"Ellie, wait." I ignore Henry's weak halfhearted plea.

As soon as the door closes behind me, I dissolve into a heap of tears. Because, from the way things are looking, Henry and I aren't courting anymore.

That's just like Henry Yoder to get me to fall in love with him and then go and pull the rug from under my feet. Is that what he's been doing the whole time? Just wooing me for no good reason?

Love? I shove away my tears and frown.

Nee, it's not love. It can't be.

For sure and certain, I do *not* love Henry Yoder!

CHAPTER 30

H ENRY

I'm a *dummkopp*, plain and simple.

And I think Ellie might hate me. Again.

Ach du liebe. What have I done?

I tossed and turned all night, not even sure I got any sleep. Even after my morning coffee, I'm still groggy and grumpy.

Ivy's interrogation after I came home so early didn't help either.

A knock on the door demands my attention.

I already know who is at the door before the second knock. I've been expecting Eli to show up and give me what for. Who knows? Maybe he'll have some sage advice for me.

I open the door and brace myself.

"Alright, what did you do this time? My *schweschder's* been crying like a *boppli* all night." Eli's frame fills the doorway.

"Really?"

Eli smirks. "*Nee.* Don't flatter yourself. But I did hear her sniffle a little and say how she can't believe she actually fell for your charms. So, I know you must've done *something* stupid."

I usher my friend inside and pour him some coffee. "I went and talked to your *dat.*"

Eli looks confused. "What? Why would you talk to my father?"

"I asked for Ellie's hand in marriage."

"Oh." Eli's expression widens. "Wait. You did?"

"*Jah,* and he said I'm probably going to have to wait for like fifty years."

"Fifty years, huh?" Eli laughs.

But it's not funny. Not to me. I want Ellie in my life. I want to see her every day. I want her face to be the first thing I see every morning. I want her kiss to be on my lips at the close of every evening.

"Well, it certainly feels like it." I shake my head. "I don't know why he just won't accept my help for the wedding. It would be *my* wedding too."

"I already told you he wouldn't take your money. I'm guessing you didn't tell Ellie, then."

"*Nee*, it's hard to be close to her, knowing I'm going to have to wait years until your folks can get caught up with their bills. And then what happens if another medical emergency occurs? I'm patient, but I at least want to marry your sister while we're still young and energetic enough to chase our *bopplin* around."

Eli frowns. "For what it's worth, I'm sorry. I wish there was a way I could help."

"I'm not expecting you to. I just, I don't know what to do."

"Have you prayed about it? Maybe *Der Herr* will make a way." Eli shrugs.

"Well, unless your *dat* swallows his pride or their bills magically disappear, I don't see a solution." I release a frustrated sigh. "And yes, I have prayed."

"Hey, are we still on for Jude's hockey game this week?" Okay, change of subject.

I nod. "Is Ellie still wanting to go?"

"She didn't say she wasn't going."

"Okay, good. Maybe I can patch things up between us. I just didn't want her to know that I talked to your father unless it was a sure thing. I was going to ask her the other day, after I talked to your *dat*, but I don't see any point in it now. Hey, Ellie, will you marry me in twenty years?" I roll my eyes.

"Well, it was fifty years a few minutes ago and now it's only twenty, so there might be hope for you yet." Eli grins.

"*Jah*, funny." I deadpan.

"If she's changed her mind about the game, I'll do my best to talk her into going."

"I appreciate that. Oh, and Jude said we should bring our hockey skates. He wants to get in some practice with us." I add, remembering my phone conversation with Jude the other day. I think he's just happy that Ivy's going to be there.

Eli brightens. "That sounds like fun."

"The driver will be here to pick us up at seven in the morning. Says that's a good time as far as missing traffic and all that. And it will give some extra time in Indy before we have to check in to our hotel. Jude says it's pretty cool there."

"Okay, we'll be here by seven on Thursday, then. It's going to be fun, *jah*? I've always wanted to see a real game in person."

"Me too."

Eli drains his coffee and stands. "Have a good day at work, and I'll try to do the same."

And with Eli's words of encouragement, I'm feeling better already.

But Thursday can't come soon enough.

CHAPTER 31

*E*LLIE

I'm perched in the back seat of the passenger van, enjoying my quiet time alone, when Henry decides to slide in next to me.

I cross my arms over my chest and frown. "What are you doing?"

"Sitting with my *schatzi*. I hope that's okay."

"Oh, so now I'm your *schatzi* again? Is that how you think it's going to be?"

"Ellie, I'm sorry about the other night. Forgive me?" He's giving me his best puppy dog look.

"Why should I? You ignored me. You didn't even kiss me goodnight!" I'm still seething.

"I shouldn't have done that."

"Then why did you?"

"*Ach*, it's complicated. I can't really talk to you about it yet." I try to ignore it when his hand glides through his gorgeous hair. Hair that I love to slide my fingers into when he's kissing me passionately.

And...I'm getting off track. I clear my throat. "Oh, well that's just wonderful. Now you're keeping secrets from me?"

"It's not like that, Ellie." He touches my hand, but I yank it away. I refuse to let him distract me.

"Then what's it like, Henry?"

He huffs. "I love you, okay? That hasn't changed. At least not on my part."

"You have a funny way of showing it."

He frowns. "The truth is, Ellie, that I'm afraid."

His words snag my attention. "What do you mean by that?"

"When I'm with you...when we're together...let's just say it's difficult for me to behave the way I should. I just want to be with you. I want you. All of you." His eyes search mine, pleading for me to understand. And I do.

Oh.

"Do you understand?"

"I think so."

"That's why I was so standoffish. I'm afraid I'm going to take us somewhere we shouldn't go. Yet."

"Yet?" *Ach*, does he mean what I think he means?

"You know, until after we're hitched. Which could still be a long way off."

"Oh." I hear the disappointment in my own voice. But Henry's right. Even if he *wanted* to marry me right away, a wedding just isn't possible with my folks' current financial state.

"It was never my intention to reject you. You have to know that."

"But I don't want to have to stop kissing you." *Ach*, there I go laying my heart out for Henry to stomp all over again. Will I ever learn?

"Good." His voice lowers, then he leans over and closes the distance between us. "Because I don't either."

And then he pulls me into his arms and kisses me full on the mouth. And my fingers get lost in that delicious hair I've been dying to touch. *Ach*, how I've missed this. How I've missed him.

A voice clears loudly, and we reluctantly break apart.

"If y'all are going to be making out, you're not doing it on my watch." Elijah growls.

Henry's eyes roam my face, like he can't get enough of me. I see fire in his eyes. "Then don't watch."

He leans toward me again, but before his lips can reach mine, Elijah says, "Alright, that's it." Then he comes and plants himself between us—or on top of us is more like it.

"*Ach*, Eli. You're such a brother!" I shove him off and Henry and I scoot apart to make room.

"I think you mean bother," Henry adds, chuckling.

"*Jah*, maybe so, but I don't have to stand for this. You wouldn't behave this way if *Mamm* and *Dat* or the deacon was here." Eli eyes us.

"None of us would be on this bus headed toward a hockey game if the deacon was here." Henry points out.

"He's got a point," I say.

"Nevertheless. You two need to be chaperoned. And no sneaking out of the hotel rooms tonight."

"Ooh, I hadn't thought of that. Not a bad idea." Henry grins, until Eli elbows him in the gut and he groans. "*Ach du liebe.*"

CHAPTER 32

H *ENRY*

I SHAKE MY HEAD, taking in the tall city buildings surrounding us as our *Englisch* driver deftly maneuvers through downtown Indianapolis.

Being in the city never ceases to amaze me. The gray buildings feel cold and resolute and yet the air holds an electricity in it as people rush along the sidewalks, some stopping at shops and restaurants, some marching on as though they walk the same path every day and are no longer affected by the sights and sounds and smells of the city.

"It's awesome, isn't it?" My beautiful Ellie grins at me and squeezes my hand, leaning toward me to get a better look out the window. *Ach*, how glad I am that Ellie and I have made amends! Having her so near thrills my soul. Her sweet scent floods my senses, and I rein in my sudden urge to remove her *kapp* and bury my face in her silky hair. And now that Elijah has finally relocated, that is actually a possibility.

Until a feminine noise distracts me and I look over to see my sister, who's now sitting on the other side of Ellie, giving me a pointed smirk. Can Ivy see the thoughts on my face? A warmth heats my cheeks and Ivy laughs. Are she and Eli in cahoots, or what?

Elijah turns around from the front passenger seat. "What's so funny?"

Ach.

"And here is your hotel!" Our driver announces, mercifully drawing everyone's attention away from myself and Ellie. He pulls the vehicle into a parking spot in front of a concrete building that must be at least twice the height of my grain silo.

I hurry to speak first. "Thanks for the ride, Mike. You'll be back here tomorrow to bring us home, right?"

The man nods. "Of course. What time?"

"Well, we're practicing in the morning, so how about in the afternoon? Maybe after lunch."

"Two sound good?"

"Perfect." I nod and pass our driver some cash. "We'll see you then."

With that, Elijah, Ivy, Ellie, and I pile out of the vehicle and retrieve our bags.

"Let's go check in. They should be expecting us." I lead the group inside and walk up to the counter. "Hi. I have a reservation for two of your rooms for tonight. The name is Henry Yoder."

After I sign some paperwork and collect our hotel key cards, we make our way to our rooms. One for Elijah and me to share and one for Ivy and Ellie. How I wish Ellie and I were sharing a room instead. But that would not be appropriate for an unmarried couple. And I certainly wouldn't trust myself. Or Ellie, for that matter. The way that woman kisses...

But perhaps the next time we're invited to one of Jude's games, that will be the case. *Jah*, right, Yoder. I try not to let the thought of not being able to marry Ellie yet dampen my spirit. *Nee,* we will all have a good time.

Thankfully, the two rooms are right next to each other. I'm happy to know that Ellie will be sleeping just on the other side of the wall. With her being so close by, I'm sure and certain I'll be dreaming of holding her in my arms tonight.

"Here they are." I announce.

I hand Ivy and Ellie the cards to their room and Elijah the extra one to ours. "Jude said we can come down to the arena any time. The game doesn't start until seven, but they will be there practicing and what not before then."

"I think we should go the arena right away. I want to see Jude and the other hockey players practicing!" Ivy has a certain gleam in her eye that makes me a little nervous. Not for the first time, I wonder just what my older *schweschder*'s feelings are toward *Englischer* Jude Riley.

"That sounds like fun!" Ellie agrees. "Perhaps we can watch them practice for a bit and then go find a bite to eat before the game starts."

"Okay then. Let's try to leave in about ten minutes. I'll call Jude from the hotel phone and let him know we're coming."

CHAPTER 33

E*LLIE*

A gasp escapes my lips as Jude flips the puck into the air with his hockey stick, sending it flying over the head of the opposing team member that has him cornered. The puck sails through the air across the rink before one of the other Icebergs smacks it down and gains control of it on the ice.

I turn to Henry in wonder. "Can they do that?"

He shrugs. "The ref isn't calling out any wrongs, so I guess so."

"That's amazing!" My focus returns to the ice just in time to see Jude's teammate skate around the back of the goal, carefully dodging the opposing players. He sneaks the puck between the skates of another player, and it slides across the ice to Jude, who is suddenly right in front of the goalie. Jude flicks the puck with his stick and sends it into the air again. It flies right past the goalie's head and into the net.

The crowd roars and I find myself on my feet with Henry and the rest of the group around us.

"Go, Jude!" Henry laughs in delight.

I throw my arms around Henry. "He did it!" I cheer.

Henry squeezes me tight, and I meet his warm gaze that absolutely melts my insides. Suddenly, I am thinking about so much more than just a hockey game.

A hand on my shoulder yanks us back down. "Come on, guys! People behind you are trying to watch the game too." Elijah scowls at us.

I shrink down in embarrassment. "Sorry!"

Henry grips my hand instead and gives me a wink. And my insides start melting all over again.

We return our focus to the game.

The buzz in the crowd is electrifying. With every trick shot the players perform, we cheer. Every time someone slips on the ice, we groan. Every time the goalie sprays his bottle of water directly onto his face, we laugh. Every time the referee calls out a penalty on the Icebergs, we shout. The fervor of the fans lights up the air in a way that is almost intoxicating.

The Indianapolis Icebergs are up, three to one, and there are only eight minutes left on the clock.

Suddenly the opposing team's goalie begins skating off the ice. He trades places with a teammate. Now there are six players on the ice, yet no goalie.

"What are they doing?" I ask Henry.

He shakes his head. "I'm not sure exactly. I didn't realize they could leave their goal wide open like that."

"That's called an empty net." A voice says from behind us. We glance back to see Sage Graves, the coach's daughter, whom Jude introduced us to earlier.

She leans forward, elbows on her knees, her eyes glued to the rink as she continues. "Any team can trade in their goalie for another forward in the hopes of turning the game around. The Hawks know they have no chance of winning right now so they're gonna push hard and get extra offense to try and score some goals."

I glance back at the rink, where another face-off is about to begin. "Do you think it will work?"

Sage's eyes flick to meet mine for just a second and I read the concern there. "It just might."

As if on cue, the puck drops, and the Hawks player snatches it away before Jude. He flings it backwards to a teammate, who takes it around the backside of the goal. A scuffle ensues. Someone gets checked into the boards. Another player pulls a one-eighty and sneaks the puck back the other direction. An Iceberg snags it away, only to have it stolen from him.

The Hawks crowd in front of the goal as the Icebergs' defensemen fight to gain control of the puck. The goalie shifts positions, standing, then crouching, making every effort to keep his body and massive gear in the way of the goal.

The puck is flicked into the air, flying toward the net.

The goalie reaches out a giant gloved hand and deflects the shot.

The crowd roars.

We rise to our feet, cheering at the victory. What an impressive save!

Then groans and shouts fill the air.

I yank my attention back to the ice and see members of the Hawks team cheering. "What happened?"

A video above the rink replays the goal. From different angles it shows how the puck was saved by the goalie. It landed on the ice just to get smacked again and sent flying back at the net. This time it flew past the goalie's head and hit the top bar of the goal, the force pushing it down into the net.

"That's called a bar down," Sage says from behind us.

Henry twines my fingers with his as we watch the play unfolding on the ice. We lean forward together, shoulder to shoulder, arm to arm, hand in hand.

The teams face off again, then battle it out, each fighting for possession of the small rubber puck. It flies back and forth across the ice. The Hawks work hard to keep it from nearing their wide-open goal. Their plan seems to be working as they manage to score another goal.

The game is now tied, three to three. Only two minutes and sixteen seconds left.

Instead of bringing their goalie back onto the ice, the Hawks continue with six offensive players. They are determined to snag another goal and win the game. They push the puck forward, seeming to inch nearer and nearer to the Icebergs' goal. A Hawk slaps the puck around the backside of the goal to his teammate. An Iceberg snatches it away and passes it to Jude, who begins tearing across the ice toward the Hawks' wide-open goal. The puck is deftly maneuvered back and forth by Jude's stick until he reaches back and smacks the puck.

It flies straight into the net. Nothing in its way.

I turn to Henry and realize we are both jumping up and down along with the rest of the crowd. My heart is pounding so loudly I barely notice the buzzer sounding the ending of the game.

"What a great game!" I can't help the massive grin stretching my cheeks wide.

Henry's bright eyes hold equal joy in their depths. Without warning, his hands cup my cheeks, and he bends down to plant his lips on mine. I kiss him back with all the fervor and excitement of the game we just witnessed—and the pleasure of being able to experience it all together with him.

Ach, how blessed I am to have Henry in my life!

CHAPTER 34

ENRY

I can hardly wipe the grin from off my face, even now as I lay on my hotel bed in the darkness.

My mind is buzzing with all the activity of the day. I can still feel the electric energy from the hockey game in my veins. I can still feel the warmth of Ellie's hand in mine as we watched the action unfolding. I can still feel the pleasure that flooded my body as her sweet lips responded to my kiss.

Ach, it was quite an unbelievable night!

I shift quietly in my bed, not wanting to make too much noise and wake Elijah.

"You awake?" Eli's voice calls from the bed next to mine.

My plan didn't work so well after all.

I turn over, attempting to see Elijah across the nightstand in the near darkness. He seems to be lying in his bed staring at the ceiling.

"*Jah*, I am awake. My mind is too busy to sleep." As though my body is responding to the very word, I yawn.

Eli sighs. "Me too."

It had certainly been an eventful night. After the game ended, we hung around and waited for the team to finish cleaning up. Jude eventually came out and greeted us all, excitedly receiving our congratulations at his excellent performance on the ice. We stayed to talk with him for a while longer before beginning the walk back to our hotel. It was nearly midnight by the time we made it to our rooms.

I wonder what time I will wake up the next morning. I am usually up before six o'clock, but I may sleep in since we are staying up so late tonight.

"Do you think we should set the alarm so we won't miss practice with Jude?" I ask.

"*Nee*, we'll wake up in plenty of time. I'm used to getting up at four. We don't have to be at the arena until nine. I think we'll be fine."

"Do you think Ellie and Ivy will want to go to a restaurant for breakfast in the morning before practice? Maybe we'll be able to walk around the city a little bit afterwards and before our ride arrives in the afternoon." I smile at the thought.

"That sounds like a good idea to me. We can play it by ear."

Maybe Ellie will find something in a shop here in the city that I can buy for her. A souvenir to bring home and remind her of this trip. She would be so pleased with me. Maybe she would even reward me with another taste of her pretty lips...*ach*, I really need to stop thinking about her lips.

EVER SINCE WATCHING THE GAME, Eli and I have been dying to get out on the ice to see how it feels to play on a real ice hockey rink instead of my pond.

Jude told us to come off the bench as soon as his teammates finish up their practice. It's kind of weird seeing him playing with all these *Englischers*. I'm so used to him being one of us. Just a country boy out on the pond. But this? This feels really big.

Especially after seeing him plastered all over the screens at last night's game. It's unreal. It's like we actually know someone famous.

And now we'll get to play with that famous person. *Jah*, it's a little strange.

Jude waves us over as the guys disappear off the ice rink.

Watching Jude practice with his teammates was fun, but practicing with Jude in the arena is a blast.

The ice is so smooth. Not to mention, we don't have to worry about the puck sailing into a snowbank and getting lost.

As usual, both Jude and Eli are on fire. I can hardly keep up with them.

We play for a while, but my eyes can't help but stray to Ellie. Oh, for the day when I can truly call her mine.

I sigh.

"Henry? You gonna play or stare at my *schweschder* all day?" Elijah's voice pulls me out of my half-conscious musings.

"What? Oh, *jah*."

"Let's take a break," Jude suggests.

I skate off to the side where Ellie, Ivy, and Sage sit. Ellie hands me a water and her smile nearly knocks me off my feet. Or skates. "Having fun?"

"Oh, *jah*. It's amazing."

"Jude and Eli seem pretty serious out there. I don't know about my brother, though." Ivy teases.

"I can't help it if I'm a little distracted." I wink at Ellie. "It's nearly impossible when the most beautiful woman in the world is watching me."

"Aww, that's so sweet of you, *bruder*." Ivy laughs.

"I was talking about Ellie. But no offense to you two. You're both pretty. She holds my heart, though." I try to explain without hurting anyone's feelings.

"That *is* sweet," Sage interjects.

"I was teasing, Henry. We all knew exactly who you were referring to." Ivy shakes her head. "Men."

I turn and see Jude and Eli talking with the coach. They seem to be in a pretty tense conversation, so I take the opportunity and sit down next to Ellie. "Sorry if I'm all sweaty."

Ellie shrugs. "It doesn't bother me."

"What time is it?"

Sage pulls out her cell phone. "Almost noon."

"*Ach*, we should probably get going if we want to grab a bite to eat and see a few sights before our driver comes." I say. "I better go get Eli."

I skate over to Jude, Eli, and Jude's coach.

"Are you sure you won't reconsider?" The coach eyes Eli.

Obviously, I've walked or *skated* in on something.

Eli glances my way, then shakes his head. "I'm sure."

The coach nods, then walks toward his daughter.

I turn to Eli. "You ready to go? We need to head out soon if we're going to eat lunch and walk around the city a little bit."

Eli nods. "*Jah*, I'm ready."

Jude speaks up. "You guys can follow me to the showers. No need to make the ladies suffer the entire ride home, right?"

"Right."

CHAPTER 35

*E*LLIE

As soon as Eli and I walk into the house, we know something is wrong.

Mamm has tears in her eyes, and *Dat's* look is positively hopeless.

Ach, not again. Gott, *please let everyone be alright.*

"What's wrong? What happened?" Eli utters the words I can't.

If it wasn't for bad luck, my family would have none at all.

Dat hands Elijah an official looking piece of paper.

"What is it?" I find my voice.

"It's our mortgage," *Mamm* says, the *boppli* bouncing on her arm.

Eli turns to me. "We have a balloon payment due next month."

"What?"

Eli frowns at the notice. "It's a lot of money." His face hardens in frustration.

"We'll need to start packing." *Dat's* voice cracks and I can't bear the pain in his eyes.

"*Nee*. We are *not* losing the farm!" Eli's voice cracks as he tosses the paper on the table and flies out the door.

I move to go after him, but *Dat* stops me. "Let him process it on his own."

I want to protest, but I obey.

Twenty minutes later, Eli is still not back so I go in search of him. I hear his voice echoing from the barn so I know he must either be on the phone or is talking to someone.

"*Jah*, I'll be there." He says, then hangs up the phone. He turns to me. "I'm going over to Henry's. I'll be back in a while."

I want to go too, but clearly Eli needs to speak with his best friend without his sister there. I give him his space. "Okay." I nod in understanding.

As Eli's buggy leaves the yard, my heart breaks a little more. I suppose I should go inside and start packing like *Dat* suggested.

If there's any way, Gott...

CHAPTER 36

H

ENRY

I'm finishing up my evening chores as Elijah's buggy pulls into the yard.

I hope he has Ellie with him, but he appears to be alone as he hops down, tethers his horse, then strides toward me with purposeful steps.

He looks like a man on a mission.

"Hey, what's going on?" I ask as he approaches.

He shakes his head. "You don't want to know."

"That's probably not true. I want to know everything, especially if it concerns Ellie."

"This does concern her, but you don't need to be concerned about it." Eli's speaking in riddles.

"What are you not saying, Eli?"

He sighs. "Forget what I said before about not being able to marry Ellie soon."

That got my attention. "What do you mean?"

"Just don't worry about it, alright? You'll be able to marry her before long. You won't have to wait for twenty years." He grins now, all gravity gone.

"Eli, what are you talking about?"

"Nothing. I have a plan, okay? I'm going to work it out. Just be patient. My folks will be able to afford a wedding soon."

"Elijah, what on earth? How? You're not going to rob a bank, are you?" I tease.

He snorts. "That's all I'm saying." He pivots, then heads back to his buggy. "Good night, Henry."

And just like that, he's heading back out of the driveway.

I don't know if I should rejoice over his words or be concerned about Eli's mental state. I mean, I'm pretty sure he wouldn't rob a bank...yet, at the same time, he didn't exactly deny it.

I shake off the ridiculous thought.

What in the world could he have planned? Whatever it is, I wish I could help him with it. Because any idea that brings Ellie Petersheim closer to becoming Mrs. Henry Yoder seems like a good idea to me. Unless it's robbing a bank, of course.

CHAPTER 37

My eyes are matted shut from crying myself to sleep.

I can't believe we're going to lose our home. After all we've done to try to get ahead, it just hasn't been enough.

On top of that, I'm concerned about my brother. Eli left to talk to Henry last night and, as far as I know, still hasn't returned.

Dat assured us last night that Eli's just dealing with things in his own way. He's the oldest of the family. He's the one, besides *Mamm* and *Dat*, who has lived here the longest.

I rise and dress for the day. When my foot reaches

the bottom step, *Mamm* is sitting at the table. *Dat* is standing next to her.

"Have you seen Eli?" *Dat* scrutinizes me.

"What? No. Not since he left for Henry's last night."

Mamm looks up at me. "He came home."

"He did? Where is he?"

"We thought you might know." *Mamm* says.

I shake my head. "I don't. Why?"

"This is from your brother." *Dat* holds up a lined paper that looks like a letter.

My eyes read the words on the page.

Dear Family,

I've signed a contract with the Indianapolis Icebergs and the hockey league, and I will be playing hockey for them for the foreseeable future. They've graciously given me a sign-on bonus as well as what I'll be making during the season. It's quite a bit.

Enclosed is money for Ellie and Henry's wedding.

I stop reading. My eyes shoot to *Dat*. "Mine and Henry's *wedding*?"

Dat says nothing, so I continue reading Eli's words.

The mortgage for the house has already been paid off, and I'll be sending payments for medical bills and the second mortgage as often as I can. We'll be able to pay those off too.

Dad, my dream is for you to be able to eventually buy back the land you sold to Ben Troyer and purchase more cattle like you've always wanted.

Mom and Dad, please rest easy now. You can keep the farm. Isn't God good? He's provided this opportunity, clear as day. You've worked so hard for our family. It is a privilege for me to give back.

Don't worry about me. After my contract has been fulfilled, I plan to come back, get baptized, and join the Amish church and settle down. Please keep me in your prayers.

Love, your son,

Elijah

"What?" My eyes scan the paper again. "Eli's playing hockey?"

And then it dawns on me. That must've been what he was talking to the coach about. Had the man been so impressed with my brother's playing and offered Eli a position on the team? I've always known Eli was really good, but this? This is amazing.

"My brother is going to play real ice hockey." I still have a hard time believing Elijah's words.

Mamm and *Dat* are both wiping away tears and I

can't tell if they're tears of sorrow or tears of joy. Maybe both?

"You're going to let him?" I'm surprised that my folks aren't more shaken up about this.

"We've discussed it. If he has signed a contract, there's nothing we can do. And it says that the mortgage has already been paid. That's not something that can be undone." *Mamm* shrugs. "We have no choice. Your brother has made up his mind."

"*Ach*, well, we *have* been praying. This must be *Gott's* answer then, *jah*?" My gaze bounces back and forth between my folks.

"At least, now, Henry can marry you." *Dat* says.

Have I missed something? I mean, I know I read about money for a wedding, but *Dat* is talking like this is something we've discussed before. I'm unsure what to make of all this.

"Henry wants to *marry* me? Did he say that?" My eyes widen.

"He hasn't spoken to you about this?" *Mamm* speaks up.

"*Nee.*"

"He came over a couple of weeks ago and asked permission to marry you come spring. He didn't want to ask you and get your hopes up if it wasn't going to be possible, you see. I told him we wouldn't be able to afford a wedding for quite some time." *Dat's* tears are back, then he lifts his eyes to mine. "But now it looks like we can. Thanks to your brother."

I wouldn't be surprised if Henry offered to pay and *Dat* turned him down. But I won't ask *Dat*, because I don't want to hurt his feelings.

For the first time since I returned yesterday, my folks are smiling, and light has returned to their eyes. They've been under so much stress lately, I'm happy they have finally found some reprieve.

I feel like giving Elijah a big, gigantic sisterly hug. I can't believe he did this. Yet, at the same time I can. He'd do anything for his family. Even if it means living in the *Englisch* world for a while.

But...there's one thing I'm still confused about.

"I'm getting married? For sure and for certain?" My gaze bounces back and forth between my folks.

"If that's what you want. You know we've always approved of Henry."

I can't help it. Joy bursts from my lips. "Oh, my goodness, I'm marrying Henry Yoder!"

CHAPTER 38

ENRY

I'm still trying to decipher Eli's cryptic message when I hear footsteps behind me in the barn. I turn and recognize an equally puzzled expression on Daniel Petersheim's face.

"Did you have anything to do with it?" His question leaves me even more confused.

Oh, no. God, please tell me Eli didn't actually rob a bank.

I set my rake against the barn stall and step closer. "To do with *what*? You'll have to explain yourself, because I have no idea what exactly you're referring to." I refrain from spouting my bank robbery theory.

Daniel's shoulders drop and he fishes out a folded piece of paper from his pocket. "Elijah left this on the table this morning." He hands the lined notebook paper to me.

I unfold it and begin reading, then stop. "What?" I look up and search Daniel's eyes for more answers but he says nothing. I continue reading the absolutely ridiculous words Eli has written. "Is this real or is it a joke?"

I would love to believe what is written, because this is *way* better than my bank robbery theory, but it all sounds like a page from a fairytale.

"So, you don't know."

"I had no clue." My eyes roam over the unbelievable words on the page. I *really* want to believe them, but I can't seem to wrap my mind around this turn of events. Dare I hope that I'll be able to marry Ellie this spring?

"Well..." Daniel just shrugs. I think he must be shocked too.

"Do you mind if I call Jude Riley?"

"Please do. This is the hockey star, *ain't so?*"

"Yes. He would know." I move to the tack room and encourage Daniel to follow me, then pick up the phone near the desk and dial Jude.

After three rings, he answers, "Hey, Henry! I guess you heard the news by now, huh?" Excitement infuses his voice.

"About Eli?" Oh, I hope it's true. Yet, at the same time, I'm not sure what this will mean for his future here in the Amish community—if he has one.

"Yes! It's one of the best rookie contracts I've heard of. They're really working with him. Coach Graves and the owners were quite generous with his sign-on bonus. I'm so excited for him and his family, and the team is stoked after watching him in practice." Jude's enthusiasm is almost tangible.

"So, it's real?"

"Yeah, it's real, my friend." Jude laughs. "And Eli mentioned something about you and Ellie getting married?"

"*Ach*, I'll need to ask her first. Then, I'll have to talk to the leaders about getting a date in the spring lineup." My face stretches in a smile that hurts.

"Well, whatever you do, send me and my mom an invite, will ya? And ask Eli for a copy of the hockey schedule so we can hopefully work around it. I really want to see you and Ellie tie the knot."

Wow, this *is* real. "*Jah*, okay, I'll do that." I glance at Daniel, his face full of expectation. "Hey, Jude, would you mind asking Eli to call his folks when he gets a chance? They'd really like to talk to him."

Daniel nods in agreement.

I hear noise in the background. "Sure, no problem.

Hey, I gotta go now. Practice will be starting soon, and I can't be late."

"Thanks for taking my call, Jude."

"Of course. Hey, I'm looking forward to seeing you and Ellie at our games. Bring Ivy too, okay? We'll hook you up with some great seats."

Excitement unfurls in my chest. "Okay, *jah*."

"See ya, Henry." Jude clicks off.

I hang up the telephone and turn to Daniel. I can't stop my smile. "It's real."

Daniel hangs his head and shakes it. "The leaders aren't going to like this. What am I going to say to them?"

"I'm not sure. But honestly, I hope they'll be happy that you'll get to keep your farm. I know losing Elijah to the world hurts, and I'm going to miss my best friend wonderful-*gut*, but his heart is in the right place. And he *did* say he plans to return. He's worked so hard to try to help you keep the farm and pay down your medical bills. I think *Gott* may have given Eli his ability to play hockey for such a time as this. We don't know all *Gott* has planned, but He does, and we need to trust Him."

"I think I need to nominate you for minister next time around." Daniel's smiling now and he cups my shoulder. "Those are words of wisdom, son. I'm thankful Ellie has found a *gut* man."

Speaking of... "Are you going back home?"

"I will stop by before I make a trip to see the bishop." His sigh exhibits the gravity of his words.

"Could you tell Ellie that I'd like to stop by and maybe take her for a buggy ride?"

Daniel lifts his knowing eyes to mine. "I can do that."

"*Denki*, Daniel."

He nods and turns to go. But before he leaves, I say, "Daniel, if you need any extra help on the farm, let me know. I'll be happy to help." Because I know the family will be feeling the void with Eli being gone.

"I'll do that." Daniel hops back in his buggy and waves as he drives away.

I release a long slow breath. This is it. I'm actually going to ask Ellie Petersheim to marry me.

Gott, *please let her say yes.*

EPILOGUE

E*LLIE*

It's been days since Elijah left to play for his hockey team and I still haven't seen or heard from Henry. I thought for sure and certain that Henry would have stopped in to visit by now to talk about...*vell*, I guess I shouldn't get my hopes up.

Just because Eli left money and said it was to be used for my wedding doesn't necessarily mean that Henry wants to get hitched this year. I swallow down my disappointment at the thought. Because lately I've been dreaming about the future. Our future.

"Ellie, Duke's all hitched up and ready to go!" *Dat's* voice booms from the bottom of the stairs.

Now that Eli's gone to the *Englisch* world, he won't be needing his horse and buggy anymore. I reckon it will be strange attending a young folks' gathering by my lonesome without him beside me. We've gone to singings together since I turned sixteen. *Ach*, I miss my *bruder* already.

When I pull up to the Beechys' property twenty minutes later, Henry is standing near the barn. Has he been waiting for my arrival?

And then it hits me. If Eli isn't here, how will his horse and buggy get home? Usually, I ride home with someone else, and Eli takes a *maedel* home in his buggy. But I won't be able to ride in Henry's buggy tonight if I have to take Eli's rig home. Perhaps I should have had Isaac drop me off.

"Is something wrong?" Henry must notice my frown as he offers his hand to help me down from the buggy. I'm careful to hold the plate of cookies—my contribution for the gathering—steady while I hop down.

His smile falters. "You *are* riding home with me tonight, ain't so?"

I nod. "I'm just not sure how I'll get Eli's buggy home."

Henry's grin returns. "I thought about that. That's why I hired a driver to drop me off here tonight."

Tension leaves my body. "Truly? You hired a driver?"

He shrugs. "I would have had Ivy drop me off, but she wasn't home."

"I see."

After an evening of singing, snacks, and indoor games due to the recent covering of snow, Henry wraps me up in Eli's buggy good and tight with the quilt and lap robe, then slides in next to me. He jiggles the reins, and we set off toward his home.

I wrap my hand around his bicep and lean in close, inhaling his scant cologne, then he drapes his arm around me and tugs me even closer.

"How's your *mamm* doing? Has she come back from Ohio?" I glance up at him from my cocoon of warmth.

A shadow passes over his handsome face. "*Nee.* It doesn't look like she'll be home anytime soon."

"So, your *grossdawdi* isn't doing well?"

"I'm afraid not. I'd really like to go see them, but it's not the right time yet."

"What do you mean?"

He looks away and scratches his cheek. "I, uh, I'll have to explain that later." Then he winks and pecks my nose with a kiss.

I have no idea what he means by that, but I drop the subject and snuggle into his warmth. I could stay here with Henry's arm around me all night and be perfectly content. As a matter of fact, I'm already dreading the moment when we have to say goodbye in the wee morning hours.

"Here we are." He pulls up to the hitching post closest to the house.

I move to get down, but he stops me. "Could you sit tight here for a minute? I need to do something right quick."

I have so many questions, but I don't ask any of them. I've learned over the past months that I can trust Henry, which is something I had never thought possible. So instead of speaking all my mind, I wait patiently while Henry enters his home. Who knows? Maybe he needs to use the bathroom and wants privacy.

A couple moments later, Henry emerges from the house again, his expression unreadable.

"*Kumm*." He holds out a hand to me, keeping the buggy flap open with the other hand. He snatches the blankets we were using. "Let's bring these in so they're nice and warm for the ride home."

I don't want to think about the ride home. I don't want to think about leaving Henry. *Ach*, how is it that this man I couldn't stand, now means the world to me?

When I step into his house, I'm greeted with a wall of warmth. One thing I've always enjoyed about our

Amish homes is having a woodstove to not only cook on, but to keep the home cozy as well.

Henry shuts the door behind us, leading me into the living room. We sink into the couch where he pins me with his captivating stare before he pulls me onto his lap and ravishes my lips with his. *Jah*, I could definitely get used to this.

Then he pulls away, leaving me longing for more. He shakes his head. "*Ach*, I'm getting distracted."

I frown. I *liked* that distraction.

He stands and offers me a hand to follow suit. I take his hand reluctantly, because I'd much rather be back on the sofa with Henry and delighting in his unabashed affection.

He tightens his hold on my hand and leads me to the hallway. And that's when I notice there is a path of lit candles that line the edges of the hallway. It's so beautiful and romantic, that I can't help my sudden intake of breath. "Henry."

We step into his bedroom, and I gulp. The last time we were in here he was...I was...we were... I still haven't lived down that moment we were caught by his *mamm* and my brother and Henry's *Englisch* neighbor, Jude Riley.

He snatches his cowboy hat off his deer rack and sets it on my head. A lazy grin forms on his face, and he makes a sound that might be a growl? Then he sobers.

"I, uh, wanted to ask you about that time in my room." He glances toward the desk drawer where he keeps his journal. "What were you doing in here? Before you, uh, attacked me."

My cheeks burn. *Jah*, I did sort-of attack him. Not that I regret it. But Henry knowing I was snooping through his private musings? What will he say? Will he change his mind about me? About *us*?

"I don't want you to get mad." I sink onto the bed and cover my face.

"Why would I be mad?" His tone is gentle, encouraging.

"Because." I rush on. "I might have seen your journal. And read it. All of it." I peek through my fingers and bite my bottom lip and wait for his explosion.

He lowers himself onto the bed next to me, removes the cowboy hat, then takes one of my hands covering my face and holds it between his own. "Really?"

I dip my head. "I'm so sorry."

One of his eyebrows arch upward. "And you don't think any less of me?"

Do *I* think any less of *him*? "For what?"

He shrugs. "For being a *boppli*. I was a mess when I wrote those words."

I take both of his hands in mine. "*Nee*, Henry. I don't think you're a baby or a mess." *Ach*, he's probably the most masculine man I know. "I think that's when I began falling in love with you."

A gorgeous smile blooms on his face revealing his straight white teeth. I still need to ask him about his toothpaste. "For real?"

I nod again, loving his vulnerability.

"*Gut*."

I rub his hand, tracing the veins with my finger. "And then you came to my house and offered to help me sew. That pretty much sealed the deal. How could I not fall in love with you? Not to mention, you're the best whoopie pie maker this side of the Mississippi." I'm only half-teasing.

He reaches under his desk and pulls out a wrapped box, then hands it to me. "For you."

I glance at the gift then study him. "It's not my birthday or Christmas."

He shakes his head and smiles. "Just open it, *schatzi*."

With hands shaking, I slide the ribbon off. "Did you wrap this?" I imagine Henry's large hands lovingly folding the paper, then clumsily attempting to tie the bow. The thought is endearing.

He laughs. "With great difficulty. It was a labor of love. I don't usually wrap things, so..." He shrugs in all his adorableness.

Ach, I don't know if I can fall any more in love with this man. I reach over and let his lone lock of hair slip through my fingers, then meet his lips with mine. "You're the sweetest."

"Open it. Please?" Is he nervous?

I finally pull off the paper, then open the box to reveal something slightly familiar. I know I've seen this clock before. I push a button on the side of the clock and a *wunderbaar* classical tune spills out. "It's beautiful."

"It's the clock my *dat* gave to my *mamm* when he asked her to marry him." His eyes are shimmering as they meet mine. "I hope you like it."

"*Like* it?" I gasp. Then, unseeing, I get lost in his pools of sea green.

"Henry?" I whisper. I can't utter anything else. This clock. This moment. This man. I know how much this means to him. I want to ask if this means what I think it does, but I'm hesitant.

Henry takes a deep breath then holds my hands in

his. "Ellie Petersheim, I've loved you for as long as I can remember. I want you in my life, in my home, every day. I want to dance with you in my kitchen. I want to take you to hockey games and share the same hotel room. I want to wake up next to you every morning and fall asleep in your arms every night. And I'm hoping that's what you want too." His eyes are questioning.

I can only nod.

"Will you marry me?" His voice cracks at the question, causing my eyes to fill once again.

I blow out a breath, then manage, "*Jah*, Henry. I will marry you. But when?"

His smile is the biggest I've ever seen, his teeth blinding. "We've got the very first date in the spring line up."

"We do? But that's...?" I mentally try to figure out how many weeks we've got.

"That's barely enough time for us to begin baptism classes, plan our wedding, and send out invitations."

Oh, my. Our lives are about to get busy.

But... "What about Elijah?"

"I already checked with Eli and Jude. It'll be tight and we won't have a lot of time with them, but they'll be able to make it."

I bounce on Henry's bed as excitement fills me. "Can we go to a game on our honeymoon? Can we have a giant mountain of your whoopie pies at our *eck* instead of a traditional cake? Can we—"

Then his lips are on mine, long and slow, sealing our promise. He finally leans back and chuckles. "Sorry. I couldn't wait another second to kiss my future wife."

"You can interrupt me for a kiss any time, Henry Yoder."

"What if you're not talking and I want to kiss you?"

"Then interrupt my thoughts."

"Your wish is my command." That adorable smirk curves up his lips before his mouth is on mine.

And *that's* how I discovered for sure and certain I DO love Henry Yoder after all!

THE END

Love Henry and Ellie's story? **Please** leave a **review** and let other readers know so they can enjoy the book too!

. . .

Keep reading for a sneak peek at the next book in the series!

SNEAK PEEK

I Might Just be in Love with the Coach's Daughter
(An Amish Hockey Rom-Com)

JENNIFER SPREDEMANN
BRANDI GABRIEL
© 2025

I skate onto the ice to the cheers of my new teammates. For the most part, everyone on the hockey team has been welcoming and seems excited to have me here.

But all I can think about is how much I miss my family and how they all must be reacting to my sudden departure. I know Ellie and Henry are happy that they'll be able to get married come springtime. But what about *Mamm* and *Dat*? Are they pleased with my sacrifice? Are they glad they won't lose the farm now?

If I had to guess, I'd say they have mixed feelings like I do. I know they'd never choose this path for my life. But when presented with the opportunity to make some real money to save my folks' farm and pay down their medical bills, I couldn't resist.

While this situation isn't ideal and I'd rather be back in my Amish community, I am grateful for this gift I've been given. I knew what I had to do the moment Ellie and I walked into the house and learned of the large payment needed to prevent foreclosure on the farm.

It was no mistake that the coach offered me a position on the team that very morning. *Jah*, I turned him down at first. But as soon as I knew we'd lose the farm without a large sum of money, I had no choice but to come talk to Coach Graves. I knew it was God's provision. Who was I to question His ways?

The Indianapolis Icebergs' head coach had been pleased that I reconsidered his offer, but we did need to negotiate a little. I only agreed to join the team if I could get the money needed to save our farm upfront. That's when Coach Graves explained the sign-on bonus to me.

Three years is a long time to be away from my family, but I can still visit in between games, practice, and training. Jude Riley playing on the team helps ease my homesickness a bit. Having a familiar face nearby is a blessing. And since we'll be roommates, we're likely to become good friends.

Now that Henry's occupied with Ellie, I have a feeling we may grow apart. Not just because of the relationship with my sister but because of the distance between us.

This new life will certainly take some getting used to.

"Hey, Pete." Eriksson swings a sweaty arm around my shoulders. "Join us for drinks and a bite to eat after practice?" I'm trying to make out his accent, but I've never been good at that kind of thing. Although his white-blond hair made me think he was probably northern European. Maybe Swedish?

Jude skates up to us. "Not tonight, Nils. He's got driving lessons." Jude has taken it upon himself to teach me how to drive so I can get my license.

That's something else I have mixed feelings about. If I get too caught up in the *Englisch* world, it's going to be difficult to find my way back to my Amish life. I already feel myself changing and I don't like it.

"You ready for your first time behind the wheel?" Jude pumps his eyebrows.

I hang my head, then nod. "I guess I have to learn some time."

Jude grins. "That's the spirit. Let's go hit the showers." He leads the way.

As we're leaving the rink, I spot the coach's daughter on the bench, and she catches my eye. I give a slight smile at the pretty brunette, then feel a strong grip on my shoulder from behind.

I turn and note Eriksson's scowl. "Best not get any ideas about the coach's daughter. We don't call him Coach Graves for nothing," he warns.

"What? I thought that's what his name is."

"It is, but it carries a double meaning. If we touch his daughter, he'll put us in our graves. Career speaking."

Oh. *Oh.* "Well, I wasn't—"

"Yeah, sure. Don't sweat it. We've all had our sights set on her at one point or another. That is, until Coach put us in our place." Eriksson grimaces. "Now, she's more like a little sister."

"I see. Well, I'll keep that in mind." When I look her way again, she's gone.

There's something about Sage Graves that intrigues me. I've never really known any women who weren't Amish, save Jude's mother, and I don't even know her well.

As I leave the locker room twenty minutes later, Coach stops me in the hallway. "Elijah."

Ach, is he going to mention his daughter and warn me off her? I gulp. "*Jah?*"

"My wife would like me to extend an invitation to you to dinner tomorrow night, if you're free." The coach must read my confusion, so he continues, "It's something we do with each new player. We'd like to get to know you better off the ice."

"Uh, *jah*. That would be great." Then I think about my driving situation. "But I don't have a car yet."

"No problem. I know where Jude lives. I can swing by and pick you up. Five-thirty sound okay?" I love how Coach Graves can immediately put a body at ease.

"Sounds good."

I blow out a breath as Coach walks away. It looks like I might get to know Sage Graves after all. And something about that thought makes my pulse race a little faster.

S AGE

Elijah Petersheim.

The name and the face—or at least those gorgeous eyelashes—have been on my mind since we first met at the game last week. I'm not sure what it is about him, but I feel like we shared an instant connection.

Which is weird, because I'd never met an Amish person before Jude's friends showed up at the game. It turns out, they're not much different than me. Of course, I only sat with their group for one game, but I felt a commonality with them somehow. I'll have to thank Jude for prompting me to help his friends feel comfortable.

When Dad said he signed on a new player, I was blown away when Amish Eli showed up. No, seriously. I literally swooned when he walked into the arena clad in his Amish attire. Most men had to work out for broad shoulders and biceps like his. But apparently, working on a farm yielded a sculpted physique that rivaled a full-time gym membership. And I won't even mention the *rest* of him.

I sigh. So, I might have a *tiny* crush on the new player.

"What was that sigh for?" Mom's voice pulls me out of my musings.

"Oh, uh, nothing." I chastise myself for getting lost in my thoughts again.

"Are you almost done with that salad?"

I glance down at the bowl. "Yes. It's ready to go in the fridge."

"Sage." Dad's voice calls from behind. "I need your help, sweetie."

I swivel toward Dad. "Anything."

"I've got a phone call that's going to take a while. Would you mind stopping by Jude's to pick up Elijah Petersheim?"

I blink. Did my dad just ask me to drive a hockey player? "What?"

"He won't bite, honey." Mom chimes in. "He's Amish, after all. I think they're good people, aren't they?"

"Yeah, but—"

"Thanks, Sugar Plum. You'll need to get going. I told him five-thirty." Dad says before he speaks into his phone and heads to his home office down the hall.

I survey my outfit. I'd hoped to at least change and apply a little bit of makeup before Eli arrives.

"Hurry, honey. The lasagna will be ready in thirty minutes." Mom reminds me.

It will take me at least ten minutes to get to Jude's

place if the traffic is decent. Which makes me wonder... what will he think of my car?

It's with these thoughts I slide into my beloved 1966 Dodge Dart.

My car brings back fond memories with my parents. They've always been into classic cars and oldies music, so I couldn't help but follow their lead. I don't know how many car shows, Hula Hoop contests, and sock hops we've been to over the years, but the culture is certainly ingrained in me. I feel like I'm a child of the sixties, even though I missed it by several decades. Heck, my parents missed it too.

As I stroll up to a traffic light, I notice a middle-aged man admiring my wheels and dipping his head in approval. That's one thing that comes with the territory of owning an oldie but a goodie. Attention—whether you want it or not.

At the next stoplight, a group of young guys look over, point, and chuckle. I ignore their ignorance and inability to appreciate a bygone piece of art. But the dig does hurt a little, if I'm honest.

The truth is, I've never really fit in with the popular crowd.

Oh, sure. I'm the daughter—adopted daughter—of a famous hockey coach. But at social gatherings I've always felt, well, awkward.

Maybe that's why I felt a connection to Jude's Amish friends. Why I feel a connection to Eli. They're different than everyone else. I noticed all the stares they received at the game. I also noticed how it didn't seem to bother them. Like they were used to it.

And that's where I'm different from them, I guess. Because I can't imagine ever becoming used to people's rudeness and prejudice.

But perhaps, maybe I could learn something from them. From Eli.

When I pull up to the curb, Elijah is sitting on the front steps of the apartment building clasping his hands. Something dark is beside him, but I can't make out what it is. Since he isn't familiar with my car, I open the door and walk around the front.

"Eli?" Man, does he look good.

Those thick lashes move upward, and he catches my gaze with his piercing blue eyes. A look of recognition passes over his face, and he stands and swings what looks like a coat over his arm. "Oh, I didn't…"

"Dad had to make an important phone call, so he sent me. Ready to go?" I do my best to still my heart and act nonchalant, but with Eli walking toward me in all his masculine glory makes it nearly impossible.

He swallows, revealing an Adam's apple I hadn't noticed before. "Uh, *jah*."

We slide into my car, and I'm inundated with cologne. Way too much cologne. Drenched cologne. I sneeze and roll down my window for some fresh air. Then I sneeze again. And again.

"Are you okay?" A concerned look flashes across his face.

"I'm sorry. I'm sensitive to smells." That didn't come out quite right.

I sneeze again.

He hands me a handkerchief. Like, a *real* one. Up until now, I didn't realize people still used them. Unless they were gang members. "It's clean."

I don't want to offend him, so I take it from his hand. "Thank you."

I blow my nose. *Way to make an impression, Sage.*

"Sorry. The spray on the bottle was broken and it kind of spilled out. I tried to wash it off my hands. I would have changed into a different shirt, but this is the only for-*gut* one I brought along." He grimaces and shakes his head.

"No, it's okay. It's probably fine for most people." I say this as I'm dabbing my watery eyes.

"Do you want me to roll down my window too?"

"Yes, please. If you don't mind. It's that crank right there."

The weather outside is a little chilly, but I'll have to

make do. It's a good thing I brought along a thin sweater.

As soon as we're in motion, the smell dissipates some and I can breathe again.

Eli's frowning and I realize I should probably put him at ease. "Don't worry. This isn't the first time. Anytime I'm in church and someone with a lot of perfume sits close by, I start sneezing."

"Would it be better if I didn't wear any?"

"No, a little is perfectly fine. I actually like that scent." Like a lot. Just not so much of it. And maybe I shouldn't have admitted that because his mouth inches up at one corner.

"You go to church?" There's a bit of curiosity in his eye.

"Yes, with my parents." I glance his way as we come to a stoplight. "Church is a big part of the Amish culture too, isn't it?"

"*Jah*." He studies me. "We meet every other Sunday. Next Sunday will be my folks' turn to host." He frowns after he says this.

"Is that a bad thing?"

"I just feel bad because I'm not there to help my folks. It takes a lot of work to prepare. Painting, cleaning, baking." He shakes his head. "I should be there to help."

"Oh, wow. You *paint* your house just for church?"

"Not the entire house. But *jah*."

"That would be weird having church at our house." I cover my mouth as I realize how that sounds. "Oh! I'm so stupid. I didn't mean *weird* weird. I mean. I didn't mean that *you* or your people are weird." I continue rambling. "Just that if a bunch of church people were to come over to *my* house, it would feel awkward."

His lips tremor at the corners, then he breaks out in a chuckle.

I gasp in mock offense. "Are you laughing at me?"

"Maybe." Amusement dances in his eyes.

"Would you like to visit our church?" The offer tumbles out of my mouth before I can stop it. "I mean, since you can't go to yours."

"I'm allowed to?" There's surprise in his voice.

"Of course. Aren't other people allowed to attend your Amish church?"

"Yes, but our community is more liberal than others. There are some communities that don't allow visitors. And most wouldn't get anything from it since the preaching isn't in English."

My lips twist. "Oh. I guess I never thought that it might not be in English."

"If visitors attend *our* church, they'll preach in both German and English."

"Oh, that's considerate." I nod. "I think it would be interesting to attend an Amish service."

He shakes his head. "For real?"

"Yeah, why not? I mean, it might be kind of strange if I was the only person there who wasn't Amish. But I think it would be an interesting experience." I would never go by myself, but if I got to sit next to Eli, and maybe hold his hand during the service, I couldn't imagine it being terrible.

We come to another light and stop. But when it turns green, my car stalls. "Oh, no. No, no, no, no, no. Not this again."

Concern floods Eli's face. "What's wrong?"

"My car stalled." I turn the key and attempt to turn the engine over. Cars behind us honk. "Oh, man. I need to get out of the intersection."

"What should we do?" He glances back at the people honking behind us as I stick my arm out the window and try to wave them around us.

"Could you get behind the car and push? I'll put it in neutral and steer." I point up ahead. "We can go to that gas station across the street, but we'll need to wait until the light turns green again."

He blows out a breath. "Okay."

"I'm guessing this is something you never had to worry about with a horse and buggy."

"*Nee*. But sometimes other things could happen. I've had my horse throw a shoe before. And one time, he freaked out when we were driving in a storm. It can be frightening."

"I guess I never considered that." The light turns green. "Okay. Hop out and push until we get to the gas station parking lot."

He nods and jumps out. I slip it into neutral as we ramble along at two miles per hour across the intersection. I sigh in relief as we pull into the gas station parking lot.

I step out and join him at the back of the car. "Thanks. I'm glad you were with me to help."

His hands slide into his pockets. "What now?"

I slip my phone out of my purse. "I'll call the tow service, then I need to call my dad and let him know why we're taking so long."

The wind picks up and I shiver.

"Should we get back into the car?" He suggests.

"Yeah. Good idea." We slip inside our protective cocoon. But without the use of the heater, it's beginning to get downright chilly.

"Are you cold? You could use my jacket." He grins sheepishly. "There's no cologne on it."

Somehow, the cologne isn't bothering me anymore. Maybe it's worn off.

"You're sure you don't need it?"

"*Jah*, I'm sure. Actually, I'm quite comfortable." He hands over his coat.

I examine it before putting it on, taking note of the thick quilting inside. The outer layer appears to be wool. "Wow, is this homemade?"

"*Jah*. Can't remember if my mom or sister made it."

It's huge on me, but I feel like I'm wrapped up in Eli's arms. I shiver at the appealing thought.

"Still cold?" His brow lowers in concern, and he beckons me near as he moves closer on the bench seat. And have mercy, his large hands rest on my shoulders and gently slide up and down my arms. His attempt at generating warmth works beautifully because my face and arms are now on fire. His assessing eyes study mine and I struggle to look away. "Is that better?"

I blink in a futile attempt to break the power his stare has over me. I force myself to nod as his hands continue to move over my arms. *Speak, mouth.* "Thank you, Elijah." I peep. "That helps."

"My pleasure." At his grin, my stomach flips a somersault. I can't help but wish that the tow truck guy takes his sweet time getting here.

I'm tempted to lean into Eli's touch. Something about his presence is just so peaceful...so disarming. Gazing into those ocean blue eyes make me want to know everything about Elijah Petersheim.

Then there's a hard knock on the window, and we scramble apart. Elijah smacks his head on the ceiling in his haste to return to his side of the car.

"Oh, dear! It's my dad."

Pre-order now!

A SPECIAL THANK YOU

We want to say a **special** thank you to **Sam L.**, who helped with research on the Amish hockey aspect of this book, readers **Janet Nush for suggesting Duke for Elijah's horse, Darlene Elbrecht for suggesting Martha for Henry's mom's name, Teena Louchart and Donna Carlson for suggesting Naomi, which we thought fit Ellie's mother well!** And thank you to **all** our readers who made suggestions. We love hearing from you!

We'd like to take this time to thank everyone who had any involvement in this book and its production, including our longsuffering **families**—especially our handsome, encouraging **husbands**, our Amish and former-Amish **friends** who have helped immensely in our understanding of the Amish ways, our supportive

pastors and **church** families, our **editor**, our **author friends**, our wonderful **readers** who buy, read, offer great input, and leave encouraging reviews and emails, our awesome **launch team** who, we're confident, will 'Sprede the Word' about *For Sure and Certain I Do NOT Love Henry Yoder!* And last, but certainly not least, we'd like to thank our ***Precious LORD and SAVIOUR JESUS CHRIST***, for without Him, none of this would have been possible!

If you haven't joined the Jennifer Spredemann Official Reader Group on Facebook, you may do so here: https://www.facebook.com/groups/379193966104149/

Are you on Instagram? Follow me here:

Thanks for reading! 😊